Love Gamble deals with topics some readers might find difficult, such as self-harm and death.

LOVE GAMBLE

CHANTAL FERNANDO

carina
press

carina
press®

Recycling programs
for this product may
not exist in your area.

ISBN-13: 978-1-335-01789-5

Love Gamble

Carina Press
22 Adelaide St. West, 41st Floor
Toronto, Ontario M5H 4E3, Canada
www.Harlequin.com

Printed in U.S.A.

For Acheron Jax,

My loving, hilarious,
beautiful inside and out third born.

I love you more, always.

Chapter One

Damon

After tipping the amber liquid into my mouth in one swallow, I place the glass down and gesture to the attractive, curvy waitress for another one. She winks at me in return, and I flash her a grin. I haven't had sex in such a long fucking time, and I'm not going to lie, I'm tempted. But now is not the time for that.

With Romeo, the president of the Angels and Devils MC, on one side, and River, his club enforcer and vice president on the other, I feel pretty invincible. It wasn't always like this, though. There was a time in the not-so-distant past when you wouldn't catch me dead sitting between these two men. After a generational war between the Angels MC and the Devils MC, the two clubs joined when the heirs got married to each other. That's right, we're living in the twenty-first century and the patriarchy is not in control. Rather Romeo and his wife, Julianna, rule together. It was a bumpy start, but by joining the two MCs together instead of fighting one another, we are building wealth and power, which is more than what we could've done on our own.

"Julianna trusts you," Romeo says, turning to look at me, his dark brown eyes missing nothing.

I nod and throw some money on the table for the next round of drinks. "I would do anything for her."

"And that's why we want you to move up in the club."

I feel my eyebrows rise. As much as this union was supposed to be a merger, it has felt like the Angels are second tier to the Devils, after one of our now ex-members killed one of theirs. This is a bit unexpected.

"How do you feel about being our new sergeant at arms?" he asks, and I can feel River's eyes on me.

Sergeant at arms. Shit. That is one of the highest roles you can have in an MC. It's the person tasked with keeping order in club meetings, securing the clubhouse, the president, and at times the enforcer. I look over to River. "Isn't that your job?"

He shrugs. "With everything we have going on and the new prospects coming in, I can't take on the responsibility of the security of the entire club and be Romeo's VP. I need help."

"And you want help from *me*?"

He side-eyes me. "You weren't my first choice," he grunts out.

I don't think he likes me much after he caught

me kissing his sister, Corey, but to be honest he doesn't seem to like anyone other than Romeo, and his woman, Bella. He tolerates Julianna.

And as for Corey...

Well, she's the reason for my recent celibacy, but I don't want to think about that right now.

"I would be honored." And I mean it. All joking aside, I'm one of the only few people who isn't part of this MC because of my birthright. In fact, I was just in the right place at the right time and got recruited. So to be working my way up the ranks so fast isn't something I really saw coming. Julianna's right-hand man, yes, but sergeant at arms?

Nope, didn't predict that one.

But I couldn't be happier about it.

We lift our glasses and clink them together in celebration, just as the doors open and five men step inside. They're wearing leather cuts, proclaiming themselves as 1% bikers, aka outlaws, and they look at us with expectation in their eyes, like they were planning on us being here.

"Who the fuck is that?" River asks, eyes narrowing to slits.

"We're about to find out," Romeo mutters, acting casual, but his body is primed and on alert. There might be five of the newcomers, but with the three of us, I like our odds. We wait to see what happens. And lo and behold, their president comes over to Romeo, while the rest of his men take a seat at the table by the door. My eyes flicker to the patch on his leather cut. It's generic—a mixture of a skull and flames. I internally roll my eyes at how basic it is.

"Romeo Montanna, I've heard a lot about you," he says, smirking. "I'm Gio, and those are my men."

"Wish I could say the same about you," Romeo replies, face hard as stone. He takes the moment to stand to his full height. River and I stay seated but are ready to spring into action if needed.

Gio laughs and shrugs. "We're a newer MC, but we've been around."

Now that he's closer, I can read his patch. *Lost Lions MC.*

I've never heard of them.

"Are you just passing through?" Romeo asks, reaching over to grab his beer and take a sip, but keeping his eyes on the man in front of him.

"Isn't that the question of the night?" Gio runs his hands through his curly blond hair. "I'm not sure. We might hang around for a bit. Is that going to be an issue?"

I can't get a read on this guy. He's trying really hard to come off nonchalant and friendly, but there is something underneath all that. I just can't place it. I look over to River and see him trying to figure Gio out as well, his brow furrowed as he studies him.

"You tell me," Romeo replies, a muscle working in his jaw. "This is our turf, and you need to respect that. If you're hanging around for a bit, cool. If you're passing through, even better."

Gio nods slowly. "We don't want any trouble,

we're just travelling around the country, trying to find our place."

"It's not here," River says from behind his president. "As long as you know that…"

"Well then," Gio says, hands up in the air, laughing. He turns back to his group, and we all share a glance.

Yeah, I don't have a good feeling about them.

But if they came here for trouble, that's what they're going to get.

The men leave before we do, and as soon as they exit the bar, Romeo turns to me. "Looks like we found your first job," he says, eyes still on the exit. "We need to handle this situation carefully."

I nod, knowing they want me to prove myself worthy of stepping up in the ranks of the MC.

"And we don't want to put the women in danger," River adds, looking me in the eye. "Or anyone you may care about."

Like his sister.

Yeah, I know what he's telling me.

I have a job to do, and I need to do it without endangering Corey.

Just another thing to add onto the list of reasons why I should fucking stay away from her.

A blonde woman approaches me, smiling and biting her lower lip.

Maybe this is just the distraction I need.

Chapter Two

Corey

I throw my paintbrush down, frustrated that I can't quite get the color of his eyes right. Just another thing that's not going my way.

And it's not like I have anyone to complain to. I've always been a bit of a lone wolf. I mean, don't get me wrong, I have my brother, River, and his girlfriend, Bella. And I have a whole motorcycle club at my back, the Devils and Angels MC, and not many people can say that. But we were born into this life and the club is all that I've ever known.

But genuine connections outside of the MC world?

Yeah, I'm lacking in those.

My father died a few years back, and I do have another older half brother out there somewhere, but I don't have anything to do with Tatum. I also don't have a close relationship with my mother. I haven't since my other brother, Matthew, died.

Maybe she wishes it was me who was murdered instead of him. We've never had that typical mother-daughter relationship, though, even when I was growing up. She was a different mother to her sons than she was to me. She was always more invested in their lives and what they were doing. She kept a distance with me. I don't know why.

I dropped out of college a few months ago, putting my business and marketing degree on hold to enjoy a slower lifestyle. I've been painting, reading, and writing. It doesn't take a rocket scientist to figure out that it most likely has to do with my brother's murder in front of me and my kidnapping a while ago. We were in a bar parking lot when my brother Matthew was beaten to death in front of me. And if that wasn't traumatizing enough, later that year I was held hostage by Rosalind, my friend's sister, when I stopped to help her on the side of the road, and used as bait so the MC would come after me. I haven't told anyone, but I have anxiety about leaving the clubhouse. I do it because I recognize that I cannot become a hermit, but that doesn't mean I like it.

I've also been avoiding asking myself what the hell I intend to do with my life. I don't know, I just feel a little lost right now. And maybe that's normal for my age. I'm just about to turn twenty.

Or maybe I'm just a fucking mess.

I think it might be a mix of both.

But I do know that I have the time to figure it out, and I will.

I always do.

Damon, one of the members of the former Angels MC, almost bumps into me at the front door, which I just opened to head outside for some fresh air. He steps aside for me to exit first so he can enter. He has a big box in his hands and dips his head at me, eyes trailing over me as he passes. "Corey."

"Damon," I reply, smiling. His usually friendly-looking mouth is flattened into a hard line, and River mentioned some extra pressure put on him by the MC. I'm not exactly sure what it's about, as no one tells me the ins and outs of the club. I do know that Julianna has closed her office, the one where they ran their real estate empire from, so everyone can just work from home or the clubhouse instead. Damon must be helping move everything out, getting ready for when we all move into the new joint clubhouse together. I step back against the wall and just watch him.

Gray eyes, dark hair, and a smile that could tempt a nun. He's possibly the most attractive man I've ever seen in my life, with a body like a professional fighter, ripped but lean, and the charm you'd warn your daughters about. And those full, perfect lips?

Yeah, I kissed those once.

My first kiss.

And probably my last from him.

I knew falling for a guy like Damon was a bad idea. Between River's overprotectiveness, my in-experience, and our ten-year age gap, all the cards are against us. Ten years isn't that much, is it? But in the rare moments we've had together, there was something between us. A spark. This time last year, I wouldn't have been able to be in the same vicinity as Damon, but now he walks into our clubhouse like it's his own. And I guess it is.

He drops the box off inside and then heads back out to his car. I can't help but admire his nice ass in his blue jeans, and the swagger in his walk. I put my paintbrush down and head out the front as he gets into his car and drives away. His energy is a little darker than it once was, but hey, I guess motorcycle club life would do that to you.

Since we shared the kiss and River got into a fight with him over it, we've kind of kept our distance.

Except for when he came to save my life when I got kidnapped, but that is a whole different story. He put his life on the line for me and then went back to being my fucking friend. Maybe not even that. Maybe after the kiss he just thought I wasn't worth the drama. I don't know. But I spend a lot of my time wondering what is going on in his mind. I know that he's been moving up in the ranks of the MC, and that he is a very ambitious man, so maybe that's part of the reason I'm not high up on his to-do list. Feels a bit par for the course in my life right now.

"What are you doing?" River asks, making me jump as he approaches from behind.

"You scared me," I groan, hand on my chest. I push off the wall and turn and look into his narrowed blue eyes, so different from my own hazel. He doesn't have my red hair either, instead a thick mop of dark locks. I've heard many women call him attractive, but not one of them has thought him approachable. The dark, menacing aura he exudes might have something to do with it.

But to me, he's River. My big brother, and the man I know would do anything to protect me.

"Is everything okay with you?" he asks, crossing his arms over his chest.

I roll my eyes and copy his stance. "Yes, everything is fine. You know, besides having no idea what I'm doing with my life."

He laughs, and I smile to myself as I notice a blue butterfly fly past us. "Corey, you are twenty. You are financially set. You have all the time in the world to figure out the rest of it."

When Matthew died, we found out he left all of his money to River and me. Matthew was responsible like that.

River gave it all to me.

So he's not wrong. But that doesn't mean I want to sit at home and do nothing with my life. I've always been a go-getter and a high achiever, so this whole life-crisis stage is quite new to me. My mother always said to me that my worth is based off my productivity, and while we don't have the best relationship, I do take that to heart. I think that is what is making this time in my life so hard for me. I just have no idea what I am doing.

"I suppose time is on my side," I mutter, smiling up at him. "Where's Bella?"

"She's on her way now—she said you two are going out for lunch?"

"Yep." I nod, taking a deep breath. Going to lunch is normal. It will be good to get out of here. "I need some girl time. No offense, but you're always around."

River laughs, and I know how much he loves that his fiancée and I are close. We're a family, and I don't think he could ever find a better woman for him than Bella. He found his match, and in doing so he also gave me the sister I always wanted. I don't know what I would do without her and Julianna. Romeo might be my cousin, but Julianna and Bella have filled the role of female friends for me. Something I was always lacking growing up, mostly due to my strained relationship with my mother.

I head back inside and grab my handbag and phone and apply some lip oil. Bella pulls up just as I step back outside.

"Perfect timing," I say as I open the door of her BMW and slide in. She looks beautiful, as usual, dressed in all black, and with her long dark hair it causes her gray eyes to pop even more. She has a striking beauty that others could only dream of. And even more importantly, she is the kindest soul.

"You know I like to be punctual," she says with a grin. She puts the car into reverse and starts to speed back down the driveway when River comes running out, so she stops and rolls her window down.

"You weren't going to even stop and say hello?" he asks, leaning in to kiss her.

I roll my eyes. Oh, how the mighty have fallen.

Most women want to bed him but are scared to stay longer than that. Where others cower, Bella stands her ground and isn't intimated by him. She brings out a softer side of River and it's made him a better person. I love him either way, but now he has a happiness about him that is contagious. And although I secretly am so happy for them both, I do love to give him shit about how much he has changed. Only when it comes to her, though.

To everyone else, he's still a sociopath.

River is the one they call when they need something done without questions. His hands might be covered in blood, but his heart is pure gold. He's protective, loyal, and deadly.

And I love him more than life.

How lucky he is, though, to have found someone who accepts him as he is. Bella loves everything about him. To her, he is perfect, and no one could ever tell her otherwise.

I only wish that I can one day find that in a partner as well.

"River, I'm starving. I skipped breakfast because I knew we were having a big lunch—I'll see you when we get back," she replies, amusement in her tone. "Not to mention I saw you this morning."

They live together. Here, with me, at the clubhouse. Bella just went to run some errands, so she had been away and busy for the morning.

They kiss again, and then he steps away from the car, finally letting us leave.

"Goodbye to you too, brother," I call out, and he laughs and waves. I catch Bella checking out his ass as she pulls out and wince. "Eyes back on the road."

"What? I'm hungry," she teases, and I shake my head at her. "Speaking of snacks, I've noticed that Damon has been around the Devils clubhouse a fair bit."

I had noticed the same thing. It's hard not to. It's like I can sense when he's around, but instead of Spidey sense, it's my vagina calling out to him. Except I get no response back.

"He's doing some stuff for Julianna," I reply, looking out the window. "And since River isn't trying to kill him anymore, I guess it's safe for him to be around now."

Probably because Damon no longer has any interest in me.

And to be honest, I'm done trying to read his mind. He knows where I am.

"I don't think anyone who dates you will ever be completely safe," she mutters under her breath.

"Well, then no one is safer than Damon," I grumble back. He hasn't made another move on me, and he's a fucking biker. If they want something, they take it.

And there's no taking going on here.

None at all, in fact.

I'm still a virgin.

And I'm not ashamed of that. I've been waiting for the right man to come along, but apparently he got lost on the way. Bastard must have my terrible sense of direction.

With a topic change about how hungry we are, the mood lightens and soon we arrive at the restaurant. I've been craving hot pot all week, and I'm so excited to be here.

"Why have I never been here before?" she asks, glancing around the tables. We take a seat and start ordering our selections on the device they hand us.

"It really is an experience," I reply with a smile, ordering some beef, vegetables, prawns, and octopus. "Do you want the hot and spicy broth?"

She shakes her head. "No, I think I'll have the laksa one."

I order more things than we'll likely finish, and we end up there for two and a half hours, chatting, laughing, and creating our heavenly hot pots. I realize as we're heading home that it's the first time in a while that I am not feeling anxious being outside of the clubhouse. I feel at peace and for once, not on edge.

When we return to the clubhouse, I'm undoing my seat belt when I hear Bella mutter, "Oh fuck."

"What?" I ask, lifting my head up.

The first thing my eyes land on is Damon standing in the clubhouse parking lot.

But this time, he's not alone.

No.

There's a tall, blonde woman with him, a tight pair of jeans hugging her every curve. And she's laughing and touching his shoulder. I suck in a sharp breath. "Who the fuck is that?" I blurt out before I can stop myself.

"I think that's the woman who is taking over our office space," Bella replies, and I can feel her eyes on me. "I didn't even know they knew each other."

I grind my teeth together as the woman plays with her hair and stares up at him. She looks nothing like me. She's a fucking Barbie, and I look like the chick from *Brave*.

He should have just said that I wasn't his type at all. Or maybe that's just my insecurity speaking. I have no reason to be angry, but I am. For some reason this has caught me off guard, maybe because he's never brought a woman around me before, or even flirted with one in front of me.

I reach for the handle to open the door, pulling on it harder than necessary.

"What are you going to do?" Bella asks, concern in her tone.

"Nothing," I force out, even though every instinct in my body is telling me otherwise. Deep inside I want to go and grab him, and ask him what the hell he's doing, and maybe shake some sense into him. "He's not mine. He can fuck who he wants."

And I don't get to have a say in that. He can be

with whoever, and I don't get to have an attitude about it. Or at least that's what I'm telling myself.

"Corey," she calls out gently as I get out of the car. She does the same and catches up to me as I walk by them to get inside.

My eyes catch his and hold in the moment I pass them, like we're in a slow-motion movie.

I don't know what he sees in mine, but he winces, slightly.

I guess I don't have the poker face that I thought I did. I've never been one to go where I'm not wanted.

And I'm not going to start now.

Chapter Three

Damon

If looks could kill, I'd be lying on the floor in a pile of ash. Bella doesn't even wave at me like she usually would, and we've been friends for years. I guess I know whose side she's on.

I don't know what I was thinking not sending Melinda away the second she showed up here. The truth is I haven't been making the best decisions as of late. I've been stressed as shit and needed some release, and things with Corey are not going to happen, for so many reasons—including her brother River, who I kind of need to get along with right now.

Add that I'm working to try to beef up security while the Lost Lions MC is lurking, potentially ready to start a war with us. Oh, and then the other things, like Corey being ten years younger and how dating her would be in strict contrast to my new role at the club as sergeant at arms. The job puts me in one of the club's most dangerous roles, and after what she went through, the last thing she should be doing is dating someone who will always put her at risk.

Oh, and also the fact that I'm a hot mess.

"Who is that?" asks Melinda, arching her brow as the front door slams shut.

I met her at the bar a few days back, and she seems pretty fun. Fun, easy, casual, exactly what I've been needing. Well, that's not true. She seemed like the second-best option, and I know it makes me an asshole for even thinking that. Desperation had me thinking with the wrong head, especially after not fucking anyone for so long. It was a coincidence she was taking over Julianna's office space, and a tie-in with the club I would have avoided if I had known.

"Women who live here," is all I say, because Melinda doesn't need to know every bit of information. And if I'm being honest, I didn't even invite her here today, she surprised me by following from the office to give me the lunch she made. Yes, I'm aware that's a big fucking red flag.

"Listen, I'd prefer it if we didn't meet here. We've only just met recently, and my family is all here," I say, rubbing the back of my neck. "So next time, just call me."

"Oh," she says, blue eyes going wide. "Of course, I'm sorry, I didn't think. I just went after you when I saw you had forgotten the food. I better get back to work anyway."

She gives me a kiss, winking at me as she walks to the road where she parked her car.

"Fuck," I whisper as I finish unloading the last of the boxes and then head inside, where I find Corey slamming cupboards in the kitchen, with Bella sitting at the dining table, softly speaking to her. Bella pauses when she sees me, so I have no idea what was being said. Corey pulls her head out of the pantry to see why Bella has gone quiet, her beautiful hazel eyes narrowing when they land on me.

"What?" she asks, scowling. "What do you want?"

"Nothing," I say, shifting on my feet. I don't want to assume that she's so upset because she saw me with another woman, but that really is the vibe that I'm getting right now. "Are you okay?"

I grimace when the words leave my lips. Yes, I want to know if she's okay, but asking is only going to make her angry—the last thing she'd want is for me to have noticed that she's pissed off right now.

She purses her lips and slams the pantry door shut. "Why wouldn't I be okay?" she asks, glaring at me dead in the eye.

I've never seen the similarities between her and her brother, in looks or in personality, but as she stares me down, an intense aura of violence surrounding her, I can see how they're related.

I shrug and bite my bottom lip as I think how to word this without setting off the already ticking bomb. "I don't know, you just seem a little angry, so I just wanted to check in on you."

Phew. I relax, thinking I did well.

"You arrogant asshole," she sneers, crossing her arms over her chest, which pushes up her perfect breasts. I try to keep my eyes on her face.

Okay, maybe not so well. Although I don't think anything I say right now would be helpful, because I'm the main target of her anger.

"What, you think I'd be angry because you're parading around my home with your new Barbie doll?" she continues, shaking her head. "Do you think you're that good-looking?"

Ouch.

I sigh. I don't want to fight with her. "Fucking hell. Sorry for asking, Corey."

I should have walked right on by and minded my damn business. I don't owe her anything. She's not my old lady. Yes, we shared a kiss a few months back, but that's it. She has no grounds to be upset.

None.

Yet why do I feel a little guilty?

"I'm going to leave you both alone," Bella mutters as she slides by me to give us some privacy. Or maybe she just wants to escape this conversation.

Hell, *I* want to escape this conversation.

Corey huffs and a lock of red hair blows off her cheek. She's fucking cute, even mad, but she's also infuriating. The cliché about fiery redheads is no joke. This woman can go from angel to the devil in ten seconds flat.

"Well, I guess there's nothing left to say, then," I

reply, crossing my arms over my chest, mimicking her defiant body language.

Seems like communication isn't our strong suit.

"I guess so," she replies.

Yet neither of us walks away, our gazes locking and holding.

The truth is, I do care for her, and I don't like the thought of her being upset. But we haven't even spoken properly in some time, and we sure as hell haven't been acting like we're anything other than friends.

If that.

If I could be with her, though, I would. The timing just isn't right. And it's not that I don't want her. I wish I could tell her that. But I guess with her seeing Melinda, it won't help anyway.

We have a silent conversation.

Her almond-shaped hazel eyes say, *There's still something between us.*

And mine say, *It's too hard, and it shouldn't be so fucking hard.*

So you want easy? her eyes reply with a smirk across her perfect lips.

We're friends, mine fire back, ignoring the dig at Melinda. This has nothing to do with her. This is between Corey and me. And I know we're not doing anything wrong. Hell, I haven't been this worked up since the last time we kissed. I've been stupid thinking that sleeping with Melinda would make me forget about Corey.

I want her.

"Fine," she says out loud, then walks past me, our shoulders lightly brushing.

Without thinking, I reach out and grab her arm, pushing her back against the wall, our bodies pressed against each other. "You look so beautiful when you're angry," I say, gaze dropping to her lips. I remember how sweet they were when I tasted them. I then remember being punched in the face by River, but to be honest, it was worth it.

"I'm not angry," she replies, but the fire in her eyes says otherwise. "And don't try to charm me. You can do what you want, Damon. I mean, you clearly are. So don't worry about me. Not that you have been."

She puts her hands on my chest and pushes. I don't move an inch. The air is so thick between us, and I don't know what I want from her. I don't think she knows what she wants from me either, but she obviously didn't like seeing me with Melinda, no matter what she tells herself.

She's jealous.

Why does that make me feel satisfied? But if she's not ready to admit her feelings, she's probably not ready for anything, right?

The timing isn't right, Damon. You have to prove yourself to the MC. And in order to do that you are going to be in dangerous situations. Being with her will put her in danger as well.

I don't fucking know.

I step away and she gets the hell out of here, leaving behind the fruity scent of her sweet perfume, and my cock hard as a rock.

"Fuck," I mutter, scrubbing my hand down my face.

No one riles me up like that woman. She makes me feel *everything*.

Maybe that's another reason I'm hesitant to give in to what I want.

It's called being smart and in control.

Right?

But I know I'll find her in my dreams tonight.

Chapter Four

Corey

An hour or so later Bella finds me in my room painting, my blood still boiling after my encounter with Damon. I don't know if he's still at the clubhouse or not, but I regret letting him see how much he affected me. I should have pretended I didn't care. He owes me nothing.

But I can't seem to forget the feeling of his body against me. His touch burned my skin and I'd be lying if I said I didn't want more.

"Can I come in?" she asks, and I nod, turning my painting around so she can't see. She sits down on my bed. "That was intense."

"I know, I'm sorry. I don't know why I got so angry," I reply, sighing and putting my paintbrush down before going to sit next to her. "I made a fool out of myself, didn't I? He's not mine—he can do what he wants."

"Maybe you should think about why you did react that way and be honest with yourself," she says, arching her brow. "It's okay to admit that you like him, and maybe you thought he was waiting for you to be ready."

I lie back on the bed with a groan. "But I am ready! He is the one who's been avoiding me!" I throw my hands up in frustration. "I assumed he was with other women, of course—I'm not an idiot. But seeing him with someone... I don't know. I wasn't expecting him to bring a woman to the clubhouse, where I live."

I'm an idiot.

I'm ten years younger than him, and today I've acted that way. I've literally proved to him why he should never want me.

"Well..." she says, biting her lip. "With the Angels and Devils joining, it's his home now, too. So you're going to have to prepare yourself." She lies back next to me and stares up at the ceiling. We will all be merging into the new clubhouse when it's ready, a fresh start for us all as one MC.

"Whose side are you on?" I nudge her. "Has he always dated lots of women?" I find myself asking. Bella came from the Angels MC and therefore has known Damon a long time.

"Not really," she admits. "I mean, I never really spent too much time around the MC back then, but I'm sure he's slept around. I just haven't seen it. And he's never introduced anyone as his girlfriend. Maybe you should ask Julianna?"

I shrug, still thinking about Damon and that woman. The idea of him touching her makes me nauseous.

Bella keeps going, not knowing about the roller coaster of thoughts I'm on. "He's usually pretty quiet and has always been so nice to all the women—he's a good friend of ours. I don't think I've ever seen him get angry before, so I was surprised by the steam coming off both of you."

"I must bring that out in him," I reply in a dry tone. "I just need to get over this. It's stupid, and if he wanted me, he would have come and gotten me. I think I've just been romanticizing the kiss, and then he was determined to come with River to save me when I was kidnapped. I thought it meant he maybe did have feelings for me."

But then he didn't make a move after that, which I should have taken as a hint.

"You know Damon's backstory, right?"

I shake my head. I assumed he was like every other biker here, who usually join through family or friends.

"His mother died when he was fourteen, and after that he was put into foster care. We met him when he was applying for a job at a restaurant we used to go to, and Paulie, Julianna's dad, saw him and had a conversation. Damon was homeless and had nowhere to go since he'd just turned eighteen. So

Paulie brought him to the clubhouse and made him an Angel. Changed his life forever," she says, giving answers without me asking, which I appreciate because I'm nosy as fuck.

I didn't know any of this about Damon, and now that I think about it, I don't know much about him at all. It makes sense now why he considers the Angels his family.

"I had no idea," I admit, brow furrowing. "What about his dad?"

"I'm not sure," she replies, shrugging. "He's never mentioned him. I'm not sure if he knows who he is."

I ponder the new information and go down a rabbit hole in my thoughts. He has an unwavering loyalty to Julianna and now, it seems, Romeo. He's a loner who doesn't quite let people in. He's kind of the equivalent of me. Except I have River.

But then I decide that I've spent enough time thinking about Damon, and I need to move on since he's already done the same.

I'm not chasing after him. He's not an ice cream truck.

"What are we having for dinner tonight?" I ask as I sit up, and she smirks at my subject change.

"We just had lunch!" she responds, and sits up with me. I start to hear music playing in the living room.

"So what? I like to plan."

Bella laughs and smacks my leg lightly. "Julianna is making a roast dinner for everyone," she explains, sliding off my bed and standing up. "You sure you're okay?"

"I'm fine," I assure her, nodding. "I had my moment, but it's done. I'm going to finish painting and then probably go for a walk or something."

She leaves me to my own devices, and I turn the painting back around to look into familiar gray eyes.

Motherfucker.

I don't generally have bad luck, but when it comes to Damon, it keeps following me. When I see Damon out the next day, again with his new girlfriend, I wonder what the hell I've done in my life to deserve this. I'd decided to go grocery shopping by myself, giving myself little tasks. But of course I'd run into Dark and Dangerous Ken and Bimbo Barbie. The only saving grace is that they don't see me, since they're eating inside, so I walk by the restaurant and go to the supermarket next door, getting the hell out of there.

When I arrive back at the clubhouse, Jag comes over to help carry in the bags. Jag is our resident hacker, the MC's man for anything regarding technology. But more than that, he's just a nice guy.

"You okay?" he asks, studying me with his intelligent green eyes. He's wearing light jeans and a beige hoodie, the hood up, covering his brown hair.

"Yeah, I'm good," I reply with a smile.

"You look grumpy," he adds, taking the two bags I was trying to carry myself, adding them to his already full hands. Being that he's a new addition to the MC, I know Jag the least, but I like him. Cute, witty, smooth. And seriously smart.

"That's just what my face looks like," I reply, smirking as I head inside with him closely behind me. He starts to help me unload the groceries, both of us working in synchronized silence.

"So what's been happening?" I ask. Even though I live here, I am not really clued in on club business. I do know something serious has been going on, though. There have been a lot of secret meetings this week.

Jag shrugs. "The usual. Just another MC in town trying to cause trouble."

Growing up in an MC, I'm used to danger, but after everything that has happened, this causes my hackles to rise.

I try to play it cool. "Is this something we should be worried about?"

"Nah, Damon thinks the Lost Lions MC will leave soon. Just need to be on guard. Hell yes," he says as he picks up the bar of Hershey's chocolate. "You are the best, you know that?"

"I know," I reply with a grin, pointing to the bag still on the floor. "And I know it's you eating all the mangoes, so I got you more of those, too."

Jag puts the chocolate bar to his chest, then walks over and bends down to give me a bear hug, lifting me off the ground in the process. "I love you."

Damon decides that is the best moment to step inside the kitchen, catching Jag and I looking at each other and laughing, me still wrapped in his arms.

I know how it looks, but I also don't care what he thinks, so I don't bother to clear anything up. At least he's come back to the clubhouse without his girlfriend in tow.

His eyes are narrowed, and he stares daggers at Jag. "Do you want River to kill you?"

"For giving her a hug?" Jag replies in an amused and surprised tone.

With Damon's tense jaw and clenched fists, it doesn't look like my brother is the one Jag has to worry about. Clearing my throat, I step away from Jag and take out the last few items and place them on the table, while the two men continue to have their standoff.

Over nothing, because nothing is happening with either of them.

Which kind of sucks, because they're both pretty hot.

Still, I'm kind of enjoying this interaction. I have to get my kicks somewhere.

Jag bites into his mango, then starts peeling it, and I'm not going to lie, I've never seen anyone eat a mango like that, but it's kind of attractive. He licks the juice off his fingers, and I try not to stare. I think Jag ignoring Damon's waves of anger only infuriates him more, and I'm here for it.

"Corey," he seethes, turning his head to me.

"What?" I ask, my tone a little more blunt than I

intend. But I'm sorry, why is he getting mad? He has no reason to be, and he should go back to his Barbie where he belongs. Okay, the truth is I'm petty as fuck, and yesterday I was jealous, but now it looks like it's his turn.

His lips tighten.

The thing between us goes deeper than just a kiss, and we both know it. When I got kidnapped, Damon made sure he was there to save me. And I knew that he and my brother would come for me.

Yet he doesn't want to admit that he wants me?

Maybe he thinks that I'm a liability after Rosalind, Julianna's sister, tricked me into thinking she needed help, but knocked me out and put me in her trunk instead.

And yeah, I hate that I was that naive and had to play the whole damsel-in-distress card, but it won't be happening ever again, let me tell you that much.

I won't be as trusting ever again.

"Yes, I thought you'd have nothing to say," I continue antagonizing him.

When he doesn't reply and give me the fight I want, I go to leave the kitchen, but stop when I pass him. "How was your lunch, by the way?"

And then I walk off before he can reply.

Fuck you, Damon.

Chapter Five

Damon

"You need to calm down, my brother," Jag says when we are alone, eating the rest of his mango. I want to shove it in his face. "If you want her, then go and get her."

If only it were that easy. I can't do that to her. There are too many obstacles standing in our way, the main being I cannot bear to put her in any danger. I've seen what Julianna and Bella have been through. And as much as I know they love their men and that it is their choice to be part of this world, I can't willingly do that. I watched my mother do it time and time again— and look where she ended up.

Dead.

No thanks.

Stretching my neck from side to side, I try to calm myself down. When I saw Jag with his arms around her, and the way he was looking at her, it just set me off.

But he's right.

"Just trying to save you from a beating," I lie, grabbing a beer from the fridge and leaning against the counter in the spot Corey just vacated.

"From you or River?" he replies, arching his brow. He doesn't seem fazed, and it's just another reminder of why he belongs here. He fits right in with the rest of us assholes.

"River," I reply, but we both know that might not be true. The smart bastard.

"Uh-huh," he comments, throwing the mango pit in the bin and turning to me. "Did she stock your favorite foods? Because she did mine."

With a cocky smirk he leaves the kitchen, while I stare at the pantry, wondering if she even knows what my favorite snacks are.

I mean, I have a few. Some are well known, like peanut M&M's and Reese's Peanut Butter Cups, and when I open the cupboard, both of them are in there.

The last thing that I've been addicted to for the last few months is butter pecan ice cream. I'm not here as often as I am the Angels clubhouse, but I did put some in the freezer a few weeks back, which I have since finished.

I open the freezer, and there it is.

Butter pecan.

I smile as I close the freezer, then walk toward her room to find her. Her living here is part of the reason I'm not around as much as I could be.

"Corey?" I call out, with a gentle knock.

She opens the door slightly. "What do you want?"

"Just to chat," I say, shrugging.

The truth is I don't know what I want, and I shouldn't be here right now. I should stay away from her, and focus on the club business, which in turn keeps her and everyone I love safe.

But for some reason I can't.

When she's around, it's hard to avoid her. I want to be near her. There is a lightness that she brings to my life. She pulls me away from the darkness.

"Chat about what?" she asks, opening the door wider. I can see her easel, and Bella's let it slip that she spends a lot of her time painting now that she's put college on hold.

"Is the butter pecan ice cream in the freezer for me?" I ask, grinning.

Hazel eyes narrow. "It's for everyone."

"It's my favorite flavor."

"I know," she replies, then winces. "It's still for everyone, though. Why are you at my door talking about ice cream? I'm sure you have other things to do. I sure do."

We stare at each other, because we both know this isn't the conversation we're supposed to be having. But I know I'm not ready for that, and then I remember her comment in the kitchen. "What did you mean by 'did I enjoy my lunch'?"

"I went to get the groceries and saw you with your little girlfriend," she explains, pursing her full lips.

"Looks like it's pretty serious. Maybe you should be hanging around her bedroom door instead?"

She closes the door, and I sigh, resting my forehead against it.

Melinda. She's supposed to be a distraction. Someone to get me to stop thinking about Corey. But it's proving to be more trouble than it is worth.

Corey sure does give as good as she gets, I'll give her that much. I need to let this…thing between us go.

"Damon?" I hear Romeo call out, and follow his voice back into the kitchen.

"There you are," he says, rummaging through the fridge. "Julianna and Julian are about to come here, and she wants you to go with her to the office one last time before she hands over the keys."

Hands over the keys to Melinda.

Julian is their son, who is only a few months old. He's the cutest little boy ever, and we all adore him. Although saying Julianna and Julian together is quite the mouthful.

"Okay, on it," I reply, glancing back toward the hallway that leads to Corey's room.

"I see Corey has stocked up the kitchen," Romeo comments, grinning as he spots his favorite beer. "I don't know how she does it, but I'm glad that she's here."

My lip twitches. "She somehow gets something for everyone."

"Who does?" Julianna says as she walks in the

kitchen, wearing an all-pink business suit. Her large handbag on one arm and her son wrapped in the other. Mother and businesswoman all in one.

Romeo reaches for both Julian and her bag and gives her a kiss. I still sometimes have a hard time wrapping my head around the fact that the head of the Devils MC fell in love with the princess of the Angels MC and joined the two clubs. They sure did turn everything on its head and managed to do it without too much bloodshed. They're lucky.

"Corey," Romeo says before nuzzling his son. Watching a biker with his child is a wild thing to see. He goes from pit bull to poodle in a heartbeat. "She went to the grocery store and stocked up for the clubhouse."

"Ah, yes. Thank god for her. Between the real estate business and Julian and the club, I'm so grateful she was willing to take over the role of looking after the clubhouse."

This is news to me. "What do you mean, take over the role?"

"Well, I'm technically supposed to be in charge of this stuff as the president's 'old lady,'" she says while rolling her eyes and giving air quotes. "But I'm leading this MC with Romeo, so I don't necessarily have time for some of the 'old lady' duties."

"Will you stop with the air quotes?" Romeo asks playfully. "You're giving me a complex. Can't you be both my equal and my old lady?"

"Nope," Julianna says, and then leans in to give

him a kiss. "I have too many titles here and 'old lady' isn't even top ten to me. Corey asked for a more active role in the MC since she's living here and wanted to pull her own weight."

What the fuck? Why didn't I know this? Why the hell would she want an active role in the MC?

Maybe you'd know if you stopped avoiding her.

My inner voice needs to go suck a dick.

"Active role?" I ask, needing to know what is going on here.

Julianna turns to me, apparently remembering I'm in the room. "After everything that happened with Matthew, we told her she can stay at the clubhouse permanently and she said she only would if she had a role in the MC since it wasn't right to stay without contributing. Romeo and I discussed it, and I knew I would not fill the stereotypical role of old lady, so I asked her to help with that stuff." Julianna starts counting on her fingers. "Make sure the fridge is always full, help me organize club events and parties, handle the clubhouse expenses, those kinds of things."

Huh. That makes sense and sounds like Corey. She doesn't like handouts. And it sounds like she's not going to be leaving the clubhouse anytime soon.

I try not to think about what that might mean for me long-term.

"Ready to go?" I ask, taking out the keys to my car.

Julianna leaves Julian with Romeo and she and I head to the office. Melinda isn't there, lucky for me, but we take the last few items and hand the keys over to one of her staff members.

"Well, that's the end of that," she comments, looking up at the building. "And now we'll make more money from the rent."

"So everyone is just working from home?" I ask, amused.

"Pretty much. We have an office set up in both clubhouses and eventually, when the joint clubhouse is ready, we'll have a massive one," she explains, tucking her long blonde hair behind her ear.

"And when will that happen?" I ask, wondering what living with Corey is going to be like. Right now, with Corey still here at the Devils', I can leave and get away when I need to, but when we're all together I'm going to see her every damn day. And now that I know Corey's here to stay, I need to figure this thing out.

Yeah, that's going to be hard.

"Most likely in a few months, when the renovations are all done. By the way, what's going on with you and the blonde?" she asks when we get back into the car.

I swear, I can't do anything around here without having to explain myself to multiple women. However, in Julianna's case, if she didn't like my woman, then there would be a problem. She's the queen bee, and her not approving would make my life hell.

"Nothing much, it was just something casual. I

saw her earlier today and told her we couldn't see each other anymore."

"Oh yeah, how'd she take it?"

I tilt my head, considering. "Fine. I mean, I didn't give her an option, but I think she took it well. She knows I'm not looking for anything more than casual," I say, reversing the car and driving off.

"Then why is she chasing after the car looking like she wants to kill you?" Julianna asks, amusement and concern mixed in her tone.

I look in the rearview mirror, and sure enough, Melinda is running after the car with a red shoe in her hand. To throw at me?

"Fuck," I grit out, and slow the car down until it comes to a stop. We're still in the parking lot, and luckily there aren't many cars around. I put the car in park and get out, just as she throws her shoe at my chest. "What the hell are you doing?"

"I fucking hate you!" she yells as she pushes at my chest.

The second Julianna sees this she gets out of the car and comes over. "You better keep your hands to yourself. He might not hit women, but I do."

Damn.

That seems to work. Melinda takes a step back and starts crying. "I hope I never see you again! You are an asshole, you know that?"

I honestly have no idea why she's so upset. She was fine at the restaurant. "I know this is an unpopular question, but what did I do?"

This makes her cry harder. "You made me fall for you!"

I'm seriously so confused. It's been a week since we met, and we've hung out maybe three times? She yells at me for about another minute before Julianna tells her, "Okay, that's enough, I think you should leave now."

We both get back into the car, and I look up into my rearview mirror to see Melinda standing there, still staring daggers at me.

"Shit," Julianna says. "Do you have a golden penis? Were you seeing her long?"

"Less than a week!" I say. I know traditionally guys are the players and the villains in these stories, but I don't understand how one week constitutes this level of response.

Julianna laughs. "Holy shit, you do have a golden penis! She must have fallen hard—and fast."

I smirk. "Thanks for having my back," I say, clearing my throat and trying to shake my confusion and embarrassment. I really wish she didn't have to see that.

"Of course," she replies. "And what is going on with you and Corey, then?"

I go silent for a few seconds, and she loses her patience. "Damon, tell me. You can trust me."

"I've been avoiding this *thing* with Corey and so when I met Melinda and she showed interest, I thought, well, maybe this will be good. Maybe I can have this thing with Melinda to get my mind off Corey."

And it had been some time, and I was horny.

"Clearly Melinda did not get the memo."

I wince. "Yeah, but in my defense I always told her I wanted something casual."

"So what happened?"

"I couldn't get my mind off Corey, despite trying."

"Oh," is all Julianna says as she starts putting everything together.

"I know," I reply, clearing my throat. "Corey saw her, and she got angry, and then I realized I still want her. I don't know. I knew I had to end things with Melinda, that it wouldn't be fair to keep seeing her, but I didn't expect this reaction."

I stay silent for a bit as I turn at an intersection, heading back to the clubhouse. "I didn't tell Corey I ended things with Melinda, because there are still other reasons we can't be together right now."

I glance over and see Julianna's eyes widen at my honesty. "Because of everything going on with the club?"

"Mostly that. I need to focus, and there's a lot of pressure on me right now. But then there's also her age, River, where we are in life…"

"Damon, I've known you for years and these all sound like stupid excuses. What's the real reason?"

Leave it to Julianna to give it to me straight.

I sigh, knowing she won't let me out of this conversation. "I know you chose this life. I know you accepted the consequences for falling in love with a biker. But it's dangerous. Corey got kidnapped and she wasn't even dating anyone in the club. I can't put her in that kind of danger. I refuse to let any woman I'm with be threatened like that. And before you say anything, I know Romeo and River accept that you and Bella made your choices. But I can't do it."

Instead of telling me I'm being stupid or that I need to let Corey choose, Julianna sits and contemplates what I just said. We drive in silence for a beat. During this time, I see a car that's following me a little too closely. All tinted windows. Turning wherever I turn.

"That's incredibly admirable, Damon. This life is hard. And dangerous. And it's not meant for everyone. But Corey was born into it. She's like me. She knows what the sacrifices and dangers are in being with a biker—"

"I could never do that to her. I know what it's like to lose someone you love when they choose danger."

And I've said too much. There's a reason people don't know much about me before I joined the club.

I take a quick look in the side mirror, careful not to alert Julianna of what I suspect and grateful that we're almost back to the clubhouse.

"Your mother?" Julianna asks in a whisper.

"Yeah. She used to work on the Strip. She met a man, fell hard, got pregnant with me. Same old story. He made her a lot of promises, but he had a wife. So my mother was a kept woman and was fine with it.

He took care of her and me, I guess. But he was in business with typical bad people. Loan sharks, mobsters, cartels. I think he laundered money for them. When I was about ten, some drama went down with his wife and my mother, and he moved us to another location, a less safe location. You know the story. Someone found out where we were, and when I was at school one day, they got to her."

I look over to Julianna, who has a hand over her mouth. My story is tragic, which she already kind of knew, but what can I do about it? My mother chose love because she thought love was all you need. I know better. She had terrible taste in men, and in the end, it caught up to her.

"You're scared, I get it," she declares. "But Damon, you can't let fear dictate who you love."

I go quiet once again. I feel kind of relieved to actually tell someone about how I've been feeling, to get it off my chest.

"So you're just going to let her think you're still seeing Melinda?" she presses, shaking her head. "And what happens if Corey moves on and starts dating someone? Then what?"

My hands tighten on the steering wheel.

"I don't understand why you're both resisting, yet secretly want each other. Or maybe not so secretly, because I think we all know."

"I don't know," is all I have to say. "See, it's complicated with Corey. And it's not with anyone else. I don't want any added drama in my life."

"That's because you don't care about anyone else like you do her," she replies in a gentle tone. "Good things aren't easy. And look, I know you're worried about putting her in danger, and I know River is difficult, and they are valid points, but you're using that as an excuse. We all make it work somehow. And the drama? Look at what just happened. That was drama."

"There's just a lot on my plate right now," I conclude. "And the safety of the club comes first."

There's definitely something between Corey and me. But am I ready for it?

And more importantly, is she?

"I can see that," she mutters, reaching out and touching my shoulder. "It's going to be okay, though. You'll both figure it out."

She sounds sure.

I'm glad someone is.

And when I still see the car following us, I know that right now is not the fucking time to start a relationship.

Chapter Six

Corey

I'm in the shower the next morning, staring at the scars on my wrist. When I lost my brother, I was at my lowest, and the scars are proof of that.

I don't hate them, though. They show me how far I've come since then, and they are evidence that I can survive anything. I'm strong. I've hit rock bottom and climbed out of that pit all on my own. Well, with the help of my therapist. No one knows about that part. If they knew…they'd think there was something wrong with me. That I need the help. And while I do, I don't want anyone to know about it. I know they would be supportive, but I don't want them to know that I'm a fucking mess. They'll start to coddle me and that's the last thing I want.

And it wasn't just losing Matthew that put me there. I got no support from my mom, who blamed me for my brother being murdered, because I was with him when it happened, and because he was defending me from the men who ended up beating him to death. I know it wasn't my fault, but I still felt guilty, and kept wondering about the what-ifs.

What if we had gone home earlier that day?

What if I wasn't at the bar at all? I shouldn't have been there. I'm not even old enough to drink. But I wanted to be included. I wanted to be an adult.

Maybe the outcome would have changed.

Maybe my brother would still be here.

Every time I see a big blue butterfly, I always think it's him.

And I've seen a few recently.

My thumb runs along my wrist absently, and I get lost in my thoughts. Grief is a slippery slope, and one thing I'm learning is that it never truly goes away, you just learn how to deal with it better. I have been better, though. I don't talk about it every single time I have a session with my therapist anymore.

And although I know River is always there for me, he's not the most emotional person, and he has this superpower of burying everything and getting on with his life. Nothing touches him, or at least that's how it appears.

Sometimes I wish I could be more like him, but I don't ever want to forget Matthew, and that pain is a stark reminder of him.

Once I'm dressed and ready to face the day, I head into the kitchen, where Julianna is making Julian a bottle, the adorable baby in her arms.

"Good morning," I say to him, putting my arms out. Julianna turns around and grins, handing him right over. "Look how cute you are in your little outfit."

"I know, right?" she replies, staring at his little face with love shining in her pretty blue eyes. "He actually slept through last night, so I feel great. I was going to come and find you—I have a proposition for you."

"What is it?" I ask, raising my gaze from Julian to her.

"I was wondering if you'd like to come and paint a mural at the new clubhouse. There's a big, blank wall, and I think it would look amazing if you brightened the place up a bit. We will pay you for your work, of course."

I knew that Julianna and Romeo had bought a place for us all to move into together, but I haven't seen it yet. The thought of being paid for my art warms my soul. I never needed recognition, but this feels like a step in the right direction. Maybe this is what I'm meant to do.

"Are you kidding me? I'd love to," I reply, smiling widely. "What do you want it to be?"

"Anything you want, but maybe something Angels and Devils themed," she replies, winking at me. "Be as creative as you like. When can you start?"

"Tomorrow? I'll go and get everything I need today," I say, my mind exploding with ideas and possibilities.

"Sounds perfect."

This is exactly what I need right now, something to occupy my mind and time. And art is like therapy to me.

I hand Julian back to his mom, and head straight to the art supply store to pick up some extra paint, brushes, and accessories. I don't know exactly what the mural will be, but I know it's going to have a bad-ass motorcycle on it. After I load everything back into my car, I go back into the mall to get an ice cream, and then find myself in a beautiful crystal store. After eying an amethyst piece, I step back and knock into someone.

"I'm so sorry," I say, turning around to apologize, my eyes widening when I realize who it is.

Rosalind.

Julianna's younger sister, and not someone I would call a friend. In fact, the bitch is one of the people who kidnapped me. Seeing her again for the first time since the incident happened sends it all coming back to me.

The feeling of helplessness.

The darkness.

The fear.

Panic.

I fight against it.

Motherfucker.

"Corey," she says, dragging out my name. "Come to check out my new shop?"

I glance around. Okay, if she wants to pretend like

nothing happened, I can play that game. It's that or get arrested for beating the shit out of her. "This is yours? Nice to see you've found a new career path—the whole villain thing wasn't working out on you."

She smirks and picks up the crystal I was admiring. "My parents bought it for me. I think I've found my new calling. Here, take this as my apology. I used you to try to get my revenge, and I'm sorry."

She opens my palm and places the amethyst in it, closing my fingers around it. "I don't want any drama. I'm moving on with my life." She spreads her arms out, showing off her shop. "As you can see."

As she disappears behind the counter, I put the crystal down and get the hell out of there, because there's no way I'm taking anything from her betraying ass. Her hatred for her older sister started when Julianna fell in love with Romeo, who Rosalind used to sleep with. Julianna had no idea about their past, as it was all kept hidden.

But some people just can't let things go.

As I ponder that thought, I get back into my car and take a few deep breaths before the drive back to the clubhouse. I'm a mess.

When I'm unloading the things from my car, Damon walks up and, without saying anything, starts to carry some of the cans of paint. I appreciate the help, and I don't have the energy to fight with him right now.

"Those can stay in the car," I explain, turning to him. "But thank you."

He nods and takes the bags from my hands instead. "I hear you are trying to make the new clubhouse look prettier."

"Something like that," I murmur as he closes the trunk and follows me back inside. "And you know I love a good art project."

"Yes, yes I do," he replies in amused tone. "I guess that means we'll be seeing more of each other."

I pause in my step for a second before I continue. "Why would you be there?"

I thought it wasn't ready for anyone to move into yet.

"I moved in—I'm setting up the security at the new clubhouse."

Does that mean I'm going to have to see him with his girlfriend?

Fuck.

I'm supposed to be clearing my head, not fucking it up further.

"I guess so. I mean, I'll be pretty busy," I say, wincing at my own unconvincing tone. He follows me to my room and puts the bags down on my bed, then decides to take a seat on top of my black cotton quilt like he lives here.

He takes up a lot of space in my room, and I suddenly don't know what to do or say.

"What?" I end up blurting out. "What do you want?"

He arches his brow, gray eyes dancing with amusement. "We can't have a conversation in your bedroom?"

I lick my suddenly dry lips. "I suppose we can. What did you want to talk about exactly?"

"You look beautiful today," he says, surprising me. "Green is definitely your color."

My fingers run down my maxi dress, and then land on the bangles on my wrist. "Thank you. Damon—"

"And your hair like that…" he comments, eying my red locks.

Okay, this is getting weird.

I'm about to ask what the hell he's on when he stands, flashes me a panty-dropping smile, and exits my room, leaving me with my jaw dropped and wondering what just happened.

If mixed signals were a person, it would be Damon.

The next morning, I'm returning from my walk when I see River and Romeo standing outside by their bikes, deep in conversation. I can see the tension practically radiating off of River. When Romeo heads inside, I approach River and give him a hug.

"Is everything okay?" I ask, reading his mood.

He sighs and looks out over the clubhouse. "There's another MC in town, and it looks like they're making themselves comfortable. Damon has eyes on them right now."

I purse my lips. "Why is Damon out there?"

River studies me a little too knowingly and shifts on his feet. "He's our new sergeant at arms, so he's going to be more involved in everything."

My eyebrows rise. "I see. So basically, he's out there putting himself in danger to prove himself worthy of the title?"

My brother's jaw tenses. "He's a biker, Corey. We're always in danger."

Maybe.

But realization hits me that he's *my* biker.

I open my mouth, then close it. "There've been other MCs around before. Why is this one so different?"

River considers my question. "They're a wild card. We know nothing about them. And with the 1%, you never know what to expect."

"What is 1%?" I've been around bikers my whole life, but they've never really explained anything to me. Matthew used to hide the dealings of the club from me, but River is very honest. He treats me like an adult, something I don't take for granted.

"The 1% are motorcycle clubs who operate outside the law. The Devils were not necessarily 1%, but we weren't law-abiding. But the Angels became more law-abiding over the years. And now that we've merged, we're definitely farther from the 1%."

"Wait, I'm confused. What does 'operate outside the law' mean? Like you do illegal stuff?"

River just gives me a look. And I internally smack myself on the forehead. Duh, Corey.

"Dumb question. Got it. Anything else I should know?"

"Be extra safe. Don't make new friends," he says, leading me back inside the clubhouse. "But we're not in lockdown or anything. We're just going to watch and wait and make a plan on getting them the fuck out of here. We don't trust them yet, so I want you to be on guard if you meet anyone new."

I nod, grateful that River is including me.

Damon is in the thick of this new mess, and I have to wonder if that's why he's keeping his distance.

Although he still had time for fucking Melinda, so there's that.

But pissing off River right now wouldn't be in his best interest, not when he's working his way up the MC ladder.

The timing isn't right, but I suppose it never has been.

Maybe it never will be.

Chapter Seven

Damon

I never thought I could be turned on by watching a woman paint. Yet here I am, unable to look away from Corey in her cute-as-fuck denim overalls as she starts to create a masterpiece on the back wall of the new clubhouse.

I pretend to continue fixing the back fence, which got damaged in the storm the other day, but I'm getting a little distracted. Especially when she bends over to dip the brush in the paint can.

I don't know why I torture myself like this. But I know I'm doing the right thing. Keeping her safe is a priority and I know something is brewing with the Lions. We've been getting reports around town, and they are getting a little too comfortable for my liking—hanging out at the local bars, getting drunk and causing scenes. They don't feel like they are just passing through, but this is Vegas.

Julianna walks out with a soda for Corey, and then walks over to me with a beer, and a smug expression on her face. "Wow, Damon. I've never seen you be so slow to fix something."

I tighten my lips, and she laughs. I'm the one they go to when they want something fixed, because I happen to be good with my hands. "You brought her here on purpose, didn't you?"

She grins and hands me the beer. "What do you mean? This is her home too, you know. And this mural is going to look epic when we have our first party at the new clubhouse next month. It isn't always about you, Damon." But her amused expression contradicts her words.

"I never said it was about me, but we did just have that conversation about her the other day—"

"Coincidence. I want the wall done, she's a talented artist, and…" She looks over at Corey as she trails off. "I think it will be good for her."

I nod, agreeing with her on that front. She's been through a lot for someone so young. Between her brother being killed in front of her, to moving into a motorcycle clubhouse, to dropping out of school.

"Now stop checking her out and hurry up with the fence. Romeo wants you at the Devils clubhouse in an hour. He's taking a few men for a ride out to deal with some business," she says, raising her eyebrows. "And River will be going too, of course."

Wonderful.

"I'll be there."

She touches my arm, smiles, and then heads back inside. I finish the fence and my beer, knowing exactly what business we're handling today.

I'm someone who appreciates the small things in life, especially after growing up in foster care. I love my family here, and I'd do anything to support them. I came from nothing. And now I've got money, power, family, and I get to ride a badass motorcycle around all day.

You sure as hell won't find me complaining.

"You heading out?" Corey asks as I open the garage door as quietly as I can, not wanting to disturb her creativity.

"Yeah, going to the Devils. You need anything?"

She tilts her head to the side and flashes me a small smile. "No, but thank you for asking."

Fuck.

I nod and step inside, grabbing my leather cut, sliding it on, and getting on my Harley.

I start the engine, enjoying the sound while I put on my helmet. I fucking love my bike. And riding her is one of my favorite pastimes. I grin as I roar off.

Romeo and River are out front of the Devils clubhouse when I ride in, standing by their bikes and chatting.

I take my helmet off and approach them. "Reporting for duty."

Romeo smirks, while River's expression gives away nothing as per usual, his blue eyes flickering.

River is a hard motherfucker, I'll give him that,

but when I see how kind and protective he is to Corey and Bella, I know that there's another side to him. It's just not reserved for the likes of me. Still, he's a useful man to have around, and he's clearly loyal to Romeo and the motorcycle club.

I was always wary of him based on his reputation alone. He was the enforcer, the one the Devils turned to when they needed to put pressure on someone. But he's not just the muscle. He obviously advises Romeo and is very strategic about how they operate the MC. I respect him, a lot.

We head off to meet with another chapter of ours, to see what they know about the Lost Lions MC.

Knowledge is power, and we need to know what we're getting into before we dive into it.

Chapter Eight

Corey

When Damon returns from wherever the hell he's been all day, I've packed up my paint supplies for the day and am sitting in the kitchen with some coffee, my own cup feeling full after a day of creating.

He glances around, then opens the fridge with an amused smile. "Making yourself at home, I see."

"Why wouldn't I?" I reply, lifting my chin. "This is my clubhouse, too."

"Yes, yes it is." He closes the fridge with his foot, hands full of ingredients. "Hungry?"

I'm always hungry. "What are you making?" I ask, intrigued.

"Nothing fancy," he replies, placing everything down on the counter. "Just some teriyaki chicken rice paper rolls with a peanut dipping sauce."

My eyes widen, impressed. "In that case, yes, I am hungry."

I watch as he works, laying thinly cut vegetables on the rolls and then wrapping them with expert precision.

"Where did you go?" I ask, nosily.

"To the bar," he replies casually, now chopping a slice of cucumber.

My eyebrows rise. "In the middle of the day?"

"Yes," he replies, giving nothing else away.

"With your girlfriend?" I press, pursing my lips.

"No," is all he says, but I don't miss the tightening of his jaw.

"Great chat," I mutter, leaning back in the chair and wondering if it's serious with this girl. Should I be writing him off completely? Why am I even thinking of that?

Shit.

I think I need to admit to myself that I've always thought that somewhere down the line, when the timing was right, Damon and I would put all of our bullshit aside and be together.

But what if this woman is his "one," just like he's mine?

What if he marries her?

After a long stretch of silence, he places a plate down in front of me with four perfect rice paper rolls and a delicious-smelling satay sauce. "What's wrong? You look like you ate something sour."

"I thought about something sour," I reply, my gaze still on the food. "Thank you, this looks amazing."

"You're welcome," he says, sitting down next to

me. He picks one up and takes a bite, and I don't know how he manages to make that look attractive, but he does.

We eat in silence, and although I'd never state this out loud because it sounds fucking creepy, I could watch him all day.

And not just because he's a literal walking Greek god, but also just the way he moves, the way he chews.

Fuck.

I need to get out of here and go home.

"I never knew you could cook," I comment off-handedly.

He grins, his dimple popping up. "I'd hardly call this cooking."

"You know what I mean," I reply, rolling my eyes. "Most of the men I know are pretty used to women doing things for them."

He pauses for a moment, as if considering his words. He then says, "I grew up in foster care after my mom died, so I've had to be pretty self-sufficient my entire life. I can look after myself well enough."

Bella mentioned this to me, but I've never heard it from him before. And I like that he's opening up to me.

"What about your dad?" I ask, saddened at the thought of his losing his family and having to grow up in the system. I can only imagine how hard that would have been. I didn't always have the best child-hood, but I did have my brothers, who have always loved me unconditionally.

"Never met him," he explains, shrugging. "And no siblings that I know of. I mean, I probably have some out there."

So he was alone. "You joined the Angels pretty young, didn't you?"

He nods. "I was barely eighteen. I met Julianna's father, Paulie, at a restaurant one day—I was there applying for a job. We got talking, and when he heard my story, he took me in. The MC has been my family ever since."

"Well, I'm glad you have all of us now," I say, trying to lighten the mood. I reach out and touch his hand quickly, then sit back and pick up my plate.

When I look back at him his eyes are locked on my exposed wrist. I know what he sees, and I know what he's thinking.

But there's no judgment in his gray eyes, only pain.

For me.

"I'm okay," I say, though I'm not sure why. Maybe because I just don't want him to think I'm in that place anymore, because I'm not.

I wish he didn't know this about me at all, but the scars are there like proof etched into my skin forever.

I'm an open book, but I'm on a different chapter now.

The air suddenly thickens as we are forced to silently acknowledge the vulnerability, heat, and connection between us.

Clearing my throat, I stand up and wash my plate. "I better head home."

"I'll see you tomorrow, then," he replies, turning to watch me. "Maybe you should message me when you get home so I know you got there safely."

"Oh, um, yeah. I can do that," I reply, my mouth suddenly dry. He wants me to text him? This is new. I suppose with the new MC about, everyone has to be more careful. I grab my bag and get out of there, sitting in my car for a few minutes to process our conversation before driving home.

And when I get there and back into my bedroom, I do as I said I would.

Corey: I'm home.

Damon: Good.

Good?

He's obviously not giving the vibes he wants to say anything further, so I leave it at that and head into the kitchen, where Bella is starting to make dinner.

"Hey, how was your day?" she asks, smiling wide. "I can't wait to see the mural."

"It was good," I reply, leaning against the marble countertop. "I'm really in my element. And I know Julianna wanted to pay me, but I'm not going to accept any money. I'm just happy to be letting my creativity out."

"She's not short on money, Corey. Just take it, you deserve it for the work you're putting in," she says, washing vegetables in the sink. "I'm going to make some salads and have the men barbecue some meat. What do you think?"

"Sounds perfect. I just ate with Damon, but I can help. What do you want me to do?" I ask, stealing the tap from her to wash my hands.

"You could make your famous potato salad," she suggests in a hopeful tone. "Or any side, really. You know we need a lot of food to feed all of these men."

She's not wrong.

I grab the potatoes out of the pantry. "Consider it done."

The men arrive and River and Romeo barbecue the meat, and then we all sit at the table together as a family to eat. Damon isn't here, and I wonder what he's up to. I know better than to ask and draw attention to the fact that I've noticed his absence. But I can't help but start to worry.

"These ribs are so good," I tell River, who is sitting next to me.

His lip twitches. "Not as good as the potato salad."

"Yeah, seriously, Corey. Marry me already," Jag teases, loading his plate up.

River throws a bread roll at his head, and Jag simply catches it and takes a bite out of it. That was pretty smooth, not going to lie.

"What?" Jag asks, chewing. "I asked her to marry me, not fuck me. I thought I was being a gentleman."

"You want to die?" River asks, eyes narrowing to thin slits. "You won't be doing anything with my sister."

"Just because she buys you mangoes doesn't mean she likes you," Bella adds, covering her mouth with her hand as she laughs.

Jag puts his hand on his chest. "Okay, ouch. Corey, tell me it isn't so?"

I try to hide my amusement but epically fail and start laughing. River watches me out of the corner of his eyes and then cracks a small smirk, too.

I know Jag doesn't mean it, and it's just his sense of humor. I think he also enjoys pissing my brother off, so he must have a death wish or something.

Or maybe he's a sadist.

I don't know, but I think he's great.

"We should have more dinners just like this," I announce, and everyone agrees.

These are my favorite kind of nights.

Chapter Nine

Damon

I rarely talk about my past, so it surprised me when I brought it up with Corey yesterday. The last thing I want is her thinking I'm just some poor little orphan boy with a dead mother and an unknown father, but I guess that's the truth, isn't it?

I know she has her own family problems and would never judge me, and maybe that's why I opened up to her so easily. Most people know the fun, smart-ass, easygoing Damon, but that's just what I show everyone. No one needs to know the story of my broken childhood. I'm a man now, and I've come so far since then. And when I finally have a child one day, I'll make sure they have a wonderful childhood.

That's all I can do. Stop the cycle.

"Good morning," I say when Julianna walks into the new clubhouse's kitchen, holding Julian.

"Morning," she replies in a singsong voice, handing me the baby. "Can you hold him for a minute?"

"Of course I can. Hello there," I say, smiling down at the next in line to this MC empire. He yawns, and I grin at just how damn cute he is. With his big brown eyes and mop of dark hair, he's actually the most adorable baby I've ever seen.

"You look good with a baby," Julianna says with raised brows. She tucks her hair back away from her face with the back of her palm, and then dries her hands on a tea towel. Once she has his bottle sorted, she takes him back.

"He makes anyone look good," I reply, grabbing a bottle of water out of the fridge. "You coming to the Devils clubhouse today?"

She nods. "Yes, I want to be there when we choose the new prospects, especially because they'll be here. It will be a little weird having strangers around here, I have to admit. It's been a while since we brought in anyone who wasn't family…"

"Yes, it has. Twelve years in fact," I say. I was the last person who was brought in.

Her eyes widen, realizing what she said. "Shit, Damon. I didn't mean—"

"It's fine," I tell her, smiling so she knows I'm not upset. "It's the truth. We haven't had any new people in here since your dad brought me in when I was eighteen."

But since we lost Victor and the men loyal to him when they betrayed us, we need some fresh meat.

And making the club bigger and stronger will only benefit us in the end. We just need to make sure that we find good, loyal men, and I think that's going to be the hard part.

Corey steps into the kitchen with a smile, her red hair pushed off her face with a black headband. She really is a natural beauty, her hazel eyes the color of a fucking amber crystal.

"Good morning," she greets, her eyes going straight to the baby. "And look at you in your little onesie."

Julianna hands him over and Corey sits down and feeds Julian his bottle, without a word passed between them. She's good with kids, and Julian looks up at her like the sun shines from her eyes. I can't blame him. And I try to push away the warm feelings I don't fucking need right now, seeing her holding him.

"I'm heading off soon," Julianna says, watching her son happily drink away. "Damon, you coming with?"

In my new role as sergeant at arms, these are the things that I need to take part in. It's a bit of an adjustment, being included in these big club decisions. "Yup, let's roll."

"We are going to meet with the new prospects. If you need anything, give us a shout," Julianna says.

"I'll be fine," Corey replies, smiling. "I'll be painting all day, and Jag is going to drop in and bring me some lunch."

"Surely Jag has other important things to do," I

say in a dry tone, the words escaping me before I can stop them.

Both women turn and look at me with varying expressions. Amusement from Julianna, and annoyance from Corey.

"Well, you take that up with your president," she fires back, pursing those plump lips.

"Come on, Damon, we better get going," Julianna says, lifting her denim jacket off the back of the chair and sliding it on. "Sorry to steal the baby back."

Corey hands him over and stands up. "I wonder if there'll be any new hotties prospecting."

I grit my teeth but ignore her comment. She truly knows how to get way under my skin.

"Yes, I wonder," Julianna replies, grabbing my arm and pulling me out of there. "Call us if you need anything!"

She loads Julian into the back of the car while I get into the driver's seat, and then she gets into the passenger side. "I swear you can cut the tension in the room with a knife every time you two are around each other. Did you tell her you dumped Melinda?"

"No."

"Oh my god," she mutters under her breath, shaking her head. "She's not going to wait around forever, Damon."

I don't say anything back, because there's nothing to say. I know the situation.

Once we're at the Devils clubhouse, we have to go to our club meeting, aka church, all of us sitting around the big wooden table to have our meeting. The prospects are waiting outside.

Julianna is the only woman present, and she's left Julian with Bella. I know she wants to push for the other women to be made official members, but she said she's going to wait until this Lions situation has been dealt with.

"I thought I'd start off with us discussing the Lost Lions MC, which doesn't seem to get the hint that they aren't welcome here. I want everyone to be on alert, and be prepared for anything," Romeo starts. "Damon, what is the update on them? Anything new?"

"We've been trailing them, and other than causing a disruption at a few of the bars, they haven't been doing much."

"Where do they go when they leave? Is it all of them that go or just a few?" River asks.

"They never go to the same place. Sometimes they go to the bar, other times on the open road. Usually to different casinos. And it's usually just Gio and two other guys. They're different each time."

"I don't like this," Romeo says, rubbing his chin. "We need to decide how long we're going to let them be here until we step in."

The room collectively agrees.

"And secondly, as you all know we've been wanting to bring in some prospects for a while now, and you were all able to nominate men that you thought would both fit in here and have the character and loyalty that the Devils and Angels MC represents," Romeo says, glancing around the table to acknowledge us all individually. "Last week we met with all of the men, and today we're going to vote on which three we want as our new prospects."

Julianna hands out a piece of paper to each of us, which is not something we'd normally do, but bringing a woman in as a leader brings a whole new level of organization we never anticipated.

"The final vote will be made by Romeo and me if there aren't any clear winners," she announces, smiling. "This is fun, don't you think?"

Romeo stays quiet, but amusement flashes in his eyes.

We all make our votes, then hand them in.

We didn't get to spend much time with each of the men, but I read their vibes, so I'm going off that. The fact that they know someone in the club too makes me trust them a little more, but I still won't be able to trust them until we get to know them properly.

There are a lot of snakes out there, more so than good people, so we need to be careful. I didn't nominate anyone, because I don't really have any friends outside of the club.

"Are they all outside waiting to be voted off the island?" Jag asks, smirking.

"No, we didn't want any fights to break out," Julianna responds in a dry tone. She lines up all of the votes, her pink-tipped nails making it look like some ASMR thing on TikTok. "We'll just let them know individually. This is the first time we've ever done something like this, so it's all trial and error at this point."

We wait as she counts them.

"Okay, so it looks like our new members are going to be, Diamond, Leif, and Blaze," she announces.

We all clap.

I'm happy with the choices.

Diamond is ex-military turned professional stripper. He's a friend of Jag's.

Leif looks like a fucking Viking and is extremely tall and built. He's new to town and wants a change from the construction job he's been working.

And Blaze is an ex-boxer. He's covered in tattoos from head to toe and has a pornstache, which he somehow makes look good.

Fresh meat.

This ought to be interesting.

And as long as they stay away from Corey, I think we're all going to get along great.

Chapter Ten

Corey

The week passes quickly, and before I know it the mural is complete. Although everyone has seen bits and pieces of it, I ban everyone from coming outside on the final two days so that the reveal will be a surprise. I cover it up with a white sheet and smile, happy with how it turned out. I'm packing up all of my things when I turn back to the sliding door, only to see a man standing there watching me, scaring the shit out of me.

"Holy shit," I gasp, dropping my paintbrush. I realize he must be one of the prospects, which Julianna warned me about.

"Here, let me help you," he says, coming over and picking it up for me. "I'm Blaze."

He grins, flashing straight white teeth. He's tall, lean, and heavily inked from his neck down, only his face remaining untouched. Dark hair, shaved on the sides, dark eyes. He'd be handsome if he didn't have a ridiculous caterpillar of a moustache sitting on his top lip.

"Nice to meet you, Blaze, I'm Corey," I say, offering him a smile before heading back inside. He follows behind and places my paintbrush on the table while I wash my hands.

"So how did you end up here?" I ask, watching him out of the corner of my eye.

"Looking for somewhere I fit," is all he replies, and I nod, understanding exactly what he means.

"Say no more."

"You're cute," he says, giving me a once-over. "But apparently off-limits."

I laugh. "You're cute too, but you'd be even cuter if you lost the pornstache."

"Never happening," he replies, amusement playing in his dark brown eyes. He runs his hand over the top of his hair. "If you don't like it then you're not the woman for me."

Of course Damon walks around the corner at that exact moment, and glances between the two of us. He turns to Blaze with a tight jaw. "Pretty sure I just told you to stay the fuck away from her."

Blaze backs down, lifting his hands. "Just having a conversation, there was no intention of anything further."

I roll my eyes. "Damon, you have serious problems, you know that? I can talk to whoever I want to. You have a girlfriend, so why don't you worry

about what she's doing instead of cockblocking me?
You just want me to be a virgin for the rest of my
life, don't you?" I don't miss the surprise in his gaze
at my admission. I turn to Blaze. "See you around."

He nods.

And I get out of there.

I don't know who Damon thinks he is, trying to
put me on a fucking shelf until he's ready for me.
This bitch needs to be eaten now, or never at all.

Literally.

I'm about to fucking expire here, while he's sleeping with whoever he wants and having lunch with
whoever he wants.

Maybe I should start doing the same and putting
myself out there. I guess before I can do that I need
to work on getting out more.

I'm done with Damon.

If he wants me, he can come and get me.

I meet the other two prospects when I storm back
into the Devils clubhouse, still angry from my conversation with Damon.

"Corey, this is Diamond and Leif," River introduces when he sees me. They're all sitting in our
lounge room, talking between themselves. "This is
my baby sister."

He emphasizes those words, the threat underneath
them clear. They aren't to mess with me.

Different clubhouse, same shit.

I roll my eyes and send him a scowl. He ignores it.

"Hey, Corey," the man known as Diamond greets me. The first thing I notice about him is he has nice biceps—in fact, his whole body is straight out of a men's fitness magazine. His eyes are a pale blue and I wonder if that's how he got his nickname. He's… sexy. There's no other way to describe him. Dark, curly hair and full lips. I mean, I wouldn't say no.

"Hey," the other man, Leif, also greets. He's tall, huge even, and I can tell that even with him sitting down. White-blond hair, Viking vibes. No tattoos that I can see.

"Nice to meet you both," I say, waving. "I'm going to have a shower and get rid of this paint."

When I go looking for Bella, she's waiting for me in the kitchen, wearing a cute linen dress and sandals, her dark hair in a long braid. "You look nice. Where did River and the two hotties go?"

She laughs and grabs her purse. "They got the tour, then headed to the new clubhouse." She lowers her tone. "Did you know that Diamond was a stripper?"

"No," I reply, jaw dropping. "But it makes sense—did you see his body?"

"I know, he's ripped," she replies, wincing. "But don't you dare tell River I said that."

"I won't and don't you dare tell Damon or River I said that, either," I grumble, tying my hair back with my black scrunchie.

She wraps her arm around me. "Your secret is safe with me. Let's go and get food, I'm starving."

After we grab some sushi, we head to the lake to sit down and have a little picnic. It's a beautiful day and it would be a shame to waste it.

"Should have brought our bathing suits," Bella says, opening her bottle of juice.

"Yeah, we should have," I reply, sliding my sunglasses down and lying back on the narrow strip of sand lining the water.

But I am still enjoying the sunlight on my skin. I close my eyes and look up toward the blue sky.

I frown when suddenly the sunshine goes away and look up to find a man standing over us. I feel my heart start to race, but force myself to remain calm. It's normal for people to talk to strangers.

"You're blocking the sun," Bella tells him.

He steps away, but still looks down at us. It's only then I notice he's wearing a leather cut. And he's not one of our men. Shit. And as I narrow my eyes to study him more closely, I realize just how fucking familiar he looks.

"I'm sorry, who are you?" Bella asks him, frowning. She moves closer to me.

"I don't want any trouble. Just saw a beautiful woman, with my sister, and I thought I'd come say hello."

I almost choke. "Tatum?"

I give him a proper look, and the man in front of me does look like my father. I don't know how to feel about this right now, but I notice Bella scooting closer to me once more.

"What are you doing here?" I ask, staring at the patch on his cut.

He's with the Lost Lions. That must be the new MC in town.

Of course he is.

"What? You don't want to get to know your other brother?" he asks, jaw going a little tight. I don't like the look in his cold eyes. He doesn't give a shit about me. And there's just a vibe about him that I don't trust.

"I'm just surprised," I reply, wanting to keep things calm between us. And I need Bella and me to walk away from this interaction safely. I don't introduce Bella. He might know her by name but not by sight, and I don't want to give away any information I don't have to.

"Are you just passing through the city?" I ask.

He shrugs and runs his hand over his bald head. "Something like that. It's pretty nice here, you know?"

"It is," I agree, swallowing hard. "Especially on days like this. You here alone?" I ask, wondering where his club members are.

He points to the café across the road. "We're getting something to eat. I thought I'd take a walk along the lake while we're waiting, and then I saw you sitting here."

Act cool, Corey. Do not show weakness.

"That's very nice of you," I lie. "And I hope you enjoy your time here."

That was my subtle "now get the fuck out of here."

He smirks and nods. "Don't you worry, I will. I'll see you guys around. Tell River that I'm looking forward to a more proper reunion."

The threat is there.

As soon as he's out of earshot, Bella pulls her phone out. "River is going to be pissed."

"That's what they want—they want to start some beef. And I didn't know why before, but I sure as hell do now," I say, turning to her. Tatum wants to hurt River, and I don't trust that he wouldn't use me to do that. "Come on, we should get out of here while we can."

We make haste and head back to the clubhouse.

I know we need to tell the men, and although nothing actually happened, I know just how this information is going to go down.

Like swallowing razor blades.

Chapter Eleven

Damon

We've all just gotten back from a ride when Corey and Bella pull in. Bella, who normally parks like a professional, turns the engine off while the car is still diagonal, and gets out in a rush. Corey does the same.

"What's wrong?" I quickly ask, giving them both a once-over to make sure they are okay.

Bella hurries inside and Corey stands next to me. "I mean, nothing happened, so don't freak out—"

"Corey—"

"We were at the lake, and some guy came over to us—"

What the fuck?

I should have been there, watching her.

"Who? What did they say? I'm going to kill—"

She cuts me off, and I grit my teeth, listening to her every word.

"It was Tatum. My brother," she blurts out, a worried look in her beautiful hazel eyes. "He's a part of that motorcycle club. I think that's why the Lost Lions are here."

I pause.

Fucking hell.

This is even worse than I thought.

I've heard about Tatum from River, but to show up here like this?

That man is either stupid as fuck or has balls of steel.

I'm thinking that it might be both, which is the most dangerous combination. A biker knows that you don't mess with the women unless you want to start a fucking war. And he's made the first move to do so.

"Why do you think that?"

"Tatum hates River. Always has. It is no coincidence that the Lions are here."

Shit. Well, that makes sense. I've been having a fucking awful time figuring out what the hell a new club like the Lost Lions wants in such a well-known area. Clubs like theirs operate in the middle of nowhere to stay undetected.

"He just chatted with us and left, so obviously he just wanted a reaction, which is apparently what he's going to get," she mutters, grabbing onto my arm. I look down at her delicate fingers on my skin. "We need to be smart about how we handle this."

"And we will be," I growl, pulling her arm gently so she's closer to me. At the same time I step toward her. "He didn't touch you? Didn't say anything inappropriate?"

She shakes her head. "No, he just said he was taking a walk and saw us and thought that he'd say hello. Do you think he was following us?"

I pull her against my chest and hold her. Imagine if something had happened to her today. I could have lost her forever. That same feeling of despair comes over me, just like when she was kidnapped. Just like when my mother died. Everything is so complicated between us, but in these moments it all becomes so simple.

"Maybe. Don't go anywhere alone without an escort from now on, you hear me?"

She pushes my chest and glances up at me with annoyance. "And who are you to call the shots on my safety, Damon? I'll be listening to whatever Julianna, River, and Romeo tell me, not you. You worry about Melinda."

Fucking Melinda.

I've let it drag out and used it as a barrier to put between us, but I'm done with that.

As she walks off I call out, "That day you saw me having lunch with Melinda was the day I broke up with her! I don't give a shit about anyone else, Corey."

That's the cold, hard truth.

And I'm done fighting it.

She stops in her tracks and turns around. "And why didn't you say anything then?" Her hazel eyes narrow to slits. "You wanted me to think you were taken, didn't you? Because then you wouldn't have an excuse to not be with me. You know what? You might be a badass biker, Damon. But when it comes to me, you are a coward."

With that blow, she storms inside, and I suddenly want to beat the shit out of something.

Or someone.

Tatum better watch the fuck out.

After a few deep breaths to calm myself down, I follow her back inside where everyone is sitting in the living room, discussing what took place.

"The women aren't to go anywhere alone," Romeo states, and I look over at Corey, and the worry in her eyes kills me. "They're fucking with the wrong club. Jeremiah and Blaze, you stay with the women. The rest of us are going for a ride."

The men all head off to prepare.

I want to talk to Corey a little more and try to explain myself, but it's going to have to wait until we get back. My eyes linger on her, but she doesn't even look at me, instead listening intently to whatever her brother is saying to her. She nods, and then takes Julian from Julianna, cradling the infant.

Sighing, I turn and follow the men to our bikes. "What's the plan?" I ask Romeo.

"I don't have a good one," he admits, jaw tight. "But I'm thinking we go find them, and then maybe just go in and beat the fucking shit out of them."

I nod, shrugging. Sounds like a pretty good plan to me.

And so we ride off in a group of black and leather, with no fucking plan, and full of anger.

Foolproof, right?

Romeo leads the way and we just follow in formation. We go down the Strip first, and finally end up at the biker bar where we first met them.

Their bikes are out the front.

They knew this is where we'd look, and it means they are expecting us. They obviously have anticipated the moves we'd make, likely based on what they'd do in the same situation.

They might have the upper hand in that sense, but this is our city, our home, and that is where they will lose.

We get off our bikes and enter the bar as a group, Romeo in the front, River to his right, and me to his left. The rest of the men are behind us.

Gio lifts his head when he sees us, and without any further warning we approach them. I look around for Tatum, but don't see anyone with the description River gave me.

"You come near our women again and it will be the last thing you do," Romeo says. His deathly calm tone is almost chilling.

"What women?" Gio replies, smirking. Tatum isn't here, so it looks like his president is going to take the brunt of the anger. "You mean those pretty little things at the lake one of my men had an innocent chat with? How were we supposed to know that they belong to you? You don't own all the women in this town, Devil."

We all know that Tatum knew exactly who we are and what he was doing.

River steps forward and stares Gio in the eye. The two of them are about the same height, but Gio is a lot wider than River.

Instead of saying anything, River just smiles at him. It's an evil smile, and it sends chills up my spine.

And then he head-butts Gio right in the face.

And then chaos breaks out.

I grab one of the men and hit him square in the nose, and from there it's just a violent outburst of punching and hitting until we hear the wail of sirens.

Then we get the hell out of there, rushing to our motorcycles.

I know it's messed up, but I haven't felt this alive in a long time, and looking around the group of men, I think that they feel the same way.

River looks over at me and smiles, blood covering all of his teeth.

Jesus Christ.

I'm glad he's on our side.

But then the sound of a bike pulling up grabs our attention. The rider is in all black and he pulls right up beside River. He turns his bike off, helmet still on, and slowly takes a riding glove off a finger at a time. Finally he pulls off his helmet and River's smile drops.

"Tatum."

The man in question, bald, with dead brown eyes, looks over at him. "Hello there, brother."

River lunges for him, jumping on him just as he gets off his bike, repeatedly punching him. The man doesn't back down, though, and gives as good as he gets.

One of the men bumps into my shoulder, pushing me back, which breaks me from my surprise, and I jump back into the pit of male ego.

They are going to regret the day they ever decided to test us.

And as for Corey?

I'm done playing games.

She's going to be mine.

Chapter Twelve

Corey

The men return looking a little worse for wear, but no one is overly injured, so I'm taking that as a win. As soon as Damon steps through the door I want to run over to him but settle for scanning him to make sure he's okay. And aside from a cut lip, he is. And although River has blood on his face and mouth, he looks okay, too.

"What happened?" I ask Damon as he approaches me in the kitchen a little later. We're alone; everyone else headed for bed while I was just finishing restocking the pantry with snacks. "I mean, besides the fighting."

"Nothing else happened," he replies, lip twitching. He watches me intensely, the weight of his gaze like a touch on my skin. "We went in there and beat the shit out of each other and then the cops came."

"Tatum?" I ask, clearing my throat.

"He and River fought hard," he admits, lifting me with his big hands so I'm sitting on the kitchen countertop, sending a shiver down my body from the unexpected contact. The way he just carried me so easily...holy shit. That was sexy as fuck.

"I've heard a little about Tatum, but you're going to have to explain the whole situation to me a little better," he says, arching his brow.

"River and I have different fathers, which River didn't actually know until recently," I say, swallowing hard. "River's dad is Romeo's dad. I'm sure you heard all about it. Matthew and I had the same father, Robert. He was an asshole. But anyway, before he met my mother he had another son, Tatum. He didn't have much to do with him at all. In fact, the first time I met him was at my father's funeral."

And let me tell you, like father like son.

My dad might not have been around to raise Tatum, but genetics won out with this one, because my half brother looked and acted so much like my dad it was like he was watching his own funeral. From the way he stood and held himself, to his cold, dead stare. I just knew he was bad news right from the get-go.

"Does Tatum know that River's actually not his brother?" he asks, eyes on mine.

I scoot forward on the countertop, my legs around his hips, feeling the tension between us. I want to look away under his intense stare, but I don't. Something has changed. I don't know when or how, but I know that the way he's looking at and touching me is different.

"I don't know. Probably not. But I know he hates River. When Robert died, he thought it was suspicious, and tried to get River pinned for it."

"Is he nice to you?" Damon asks, trying to piece together our extremely dysfunctional family situation. "Do you care about him at all?"

"No," I admit, shrugging. "When I first met him at the funeral, he wasn't mean or anything, just indifferent. We don't have any kind of relationship. I don't consider him my family, at all. This is only the second time I've ever seen him in my whole life. We're pretty much strangers."

As far as I'm concerned, River is the only brother I have left. He has always been there for me, and loved and protected me.

He's my family.

"I think he's here because of River. There is something there and I just know it's because of River," I say.

Damon's thumb starts to rub circles on my thigh, and I can barely think straight.

"Well, at least we can try to understand their motive now. Before we had no idea what they were up to," he replies, stopping and just studying me a little too closely with…gentleness in his eyes. And also a little heat. He strokes the side of my face and my breath hitches.

What the actual fuck.

"Are you drunk or something?" I ask, eyes narrowing. "You're acting weird."

Anyone could walk into this kitchen at any moment and see him all up in my grill, leaning over me, our faces close enough that I can see the speckles of blue in his gray eyes.

"No," he replies, sighing. "I'm not drunk, Corey. I just think that I'm finally seeing things in a different light. Tomorrow isn't really promised to everyone. Hell, I could die this next week. Who knows? But I don't want to leave this earth without tasting you, fucking you, and making you mine. I think that would be my only regret."

My jaw drops open.

I cannot believe the words coming out of his mouth, and I can't even form a witty or sexy reply because I'm about to have a heart attack.

And then Bella walks in and stops when she sees us. "Oh, sorry. I'm just going to…uh…"

Damon steps back, his lip twitching. And then he moves back to me and kisses my forehead before leaving the kitchen.

"What was that?" she asks, watching him walk away with her brow furrowed. "Did he just kiss you?"

"Yes, he did. I don't know what that was," I admit, jumping down from the counter and staring at the now empty doorway. "But I think that he's had an epiphany of some kind. He doesn't have the best timing—we're in a crisis right now."

"I guess crisis mode brings out certain things in

people. And I'm sorry I interrupted your moment," she says, grinning as she pulls out a chair and sits down. "But I will say that you're lucky it's me and not River that came in to get us a drink."

I sit down next to her. "Is this my main character moment? I feel like it might be."

Oh my god.

Damon is finally *seeing* me.

I mean, really seeing me.

What is going on in that head of his? Why now?

I can't deny the fact that I feel…good about this. Really fucking good.

Bella takes my hand in her and squeals. "Okay, tell me everything!"

It might not be much, but she knows how long I've been waiting for Damon to finally stake his claim on me. And while that might not have been that exactly, it was still way more than he's given me since our kiss.

There's not much to tell, but I share it all anyway.

And we do a happy dance together, forgetting about all the other stress in our world right now.

"Now when are you revealing your mural?" she then asks.

With all the chaos, I'd almost forgotten about that. "Maybe we could do it tomorrow? We can invite everyone over for dinner. I think it's nice for us to all be together while shit is hitting the fan."

I just hope Tatum doesn't do anything stupid. I

couldn't bear it if anything happened to Damon or River.

"Sounds perfect. I'll organize some food," she replies, tucking her dark hair back behind her ear. "And I'll send out a group message."

How wild the biker world is—a group fight today and a party tomorrow.

But just like that, things are looking up.

And maybe I won't be dying a virgin.

Chapter Thirteen

Damon

The next time I see Corey is at her mural reveal party. I've been waiting to see the finished version ever since I've seen her working on it here and there, and although the timing isn't great, for her I'm trying to act calm and let go of the pressure I'm carrying right now. Between trying to gather more intel on the Lost Lions MC and making sure we're on high alert, I'm a walking stress ball.

The women have gone all out as usual, with plenty of food, drinks, and good music. I suppose it's kept them busy and distracted today, which is a good thing. This is the first party the prospects will be attending, and although it's probably going to be a little more family-oriented than they'd be expecting, it's still going to be a good night with all of us together. However, we're all still on alert, and taking turns checking the perimeter and cameras.

Corey comes out in tight ripped jeans, black heeled boots, and a white crop top, showing off her stomach. "You look beautiful," I tell her when she approaches me.

It feels great to finally tell her this. To finally go after what I want.

I don't care: whatever is standing in our way, we will handle. The timing is never going to be right, and I've been kidding myself thinking I can just leave her alone, even if it might be the easier option.

Easy never gets you anything.

She smiles and looks down, her long eyelashes fanning on her cheeks. "Thank you, Damon. You've been full of compliments lately."

"We need to have a chat. Tonight?"

I want everything out on the table. I want to tell her how I feel and explain to her why I was so hesitant to admit that I want her. I want her to know where my mind has been at, and I want to know her thoughts, too.

"Sure." She nods, and I take her hand in mine.

"Do you need me to do anything?"

"Um, you could carry out the last platter," she says, pointing to a big wooden board filled with everything from cold meats to fruit and dips.

"On it." I carry the platter out and place it with the rest of them. Whoever made all of this took a lot of time. I pick up a kiwi fruit in the shape of a star and inspect it.

"Pretty cool, hey?" Julianna says, picking up a

strawberry and taking a bite. "We found a caterer to do it all because we couldn't be bothered."

I laugh. "And fair enough. It all looks amazing."

After about an hour, we all gather in front of the back wall, draped with a large white sheet, and look up.

"I just wanted to thank Julianna for letting me paint my little heart out," Corey says to the crowd, one hand on the sheet. "And yeah, I hope you all like it."

She pulls down and shows us all what she's been working on.

And it's incredible.

I knew she was talented, but this piece of art is mind-blowing. There's a big black Harley in the middle, the details so intricate, so perfect, and it's parked on a painted road. One side has a lake and the other a sparse desert and on the bottom right corner it says *Devils and Angels MC: Together We are Stronger.*

And on closer inspection, I understand why I love the bike so much.

It's mine.

She's painted an exact replica of my treasured motorcycle.

I think I'm in fucking love.

We all clap and cheer and admire, and I'm the loudest, I don't care. I stand back, letting everyone congratulate her first. As the crowd around her dies, I stalk toward her.

"You are so talented," I tell her, my tone filled with pride. "That's my bike, isn't it?"

She ducks her face, but her pretty smile tells me all the answers that I need.

"I love it so much," I add.

"Thank you," she replies, glancing up at it. "I'm pretty happy with it."

"You kidding? It's unbelievable. You should learn how to tattoo because I'd let those hands all over my body," I say, grinning at her blush.

"Corey, you are amazing, girl," Julianna says as she approaches, hugging her warmly. "I love it so much. I knew I would."

"I'm glad," Corey says, beaming at the compliments. "I'm going to get a drink. I think I deserve one."

She heads to the bar, and I watch her walk away. "What's going on with you two?" Julianna asks when we are alone.

"Nothing. Yet," I reply, turning back to her. "But I've decided I don't care about any of it. The age gap, River. I want her. I can't stop thinking about her. I'm done fighting it."

I'll take whatever River wants to throw my way.

Julianna smiles widely. "There are no rules in love and war."

"Now I just need to either speak to River and get his approval, or fight him to the death," I mutter.

"The latter is probably your best bet, then," she jokes, her blue eyes dancing with amusement as she looks over at the man in question. "He can't expect Corey to stay single forever. She's a grown adult. But the whole situation with Tatum has him more on edge right now, so it might not be the best time to let him know you want to take his baby sister's virginity."

"Okay, maybe don't say that so loud," I say, also because the thought of it makes me hard. "It's about a lot more than that with her. I don't care if she's been with other men or not. I just want her."

"Well, that was cute, and it's so nice to hear you finally admitting to this," Julianna says, turning when Romeo approaches, Julian in his arms.

"What are you whispering about over here?" he asks, eyes still on his son.

"Nothing," we both say at the same time, then start laughing.

Romeo looks at his wife. "Julianna—"

He's going to know soon enough anyway, so I might as well tell him, I decide. "I want to make Corey my old lady."

Romeo's mouth opens, then closes. Finally, he mutters a curse. "You have a set of balls on you, Damon."

"I know, and I know you all don't need the extra drama, but I've thought about it and sat on it, and life's just too short to live my life for other people," I explain, hoping he understands. "Being with her isn't going to hurt anyone, and surely River would want her with a brother instead of some other man."

"I don't think he wants her with anyone," he replies in a dry tone, slapping my shoulder with an amused grin. "But I hear you. The heart wants what the heart wants. And you're right, you're a good man. She could do worse. Your timing is pretty fucked, though. River is worried that Tatum might hurt Corey to get to him, so he's not in the best of moods."

No one is going to hurt Corey.

Ever.

"He's never in a good mood," I grumble, and Romeo simply laughs.

"Attaching Corey to a high-ranking member sounds like a good plan to me. You'd protect her, and what more could River ask for?"

"I hope he sees it that same way," I reply, and Romeo just grins and hands me his son.

"Can you hold him? I'm going to have a dance with my beautiful wife."

He whisks her away and I look down into a now sleeping baby's adorable face.

Smiling, I whisper, "You have it easy, you know that?"

Chapter Fourteen

Corey

Watching Damon holding Julian, my heart melts a little, and if I wanted to have children, I'm sure my ovaries would be bursting.

"He's so good with him," Julianna comments after she finishes her dance. "Look, he's singing and dancing with him now."

I know Julianna and Damon are close and that he probably talks to her about things. So I ask her, "What do you know?"

She laughs. "About what?"

"About how Damon feels about me," I reply boldly, turning to face her and blocking her view of him. "First I was getting all the signals, then mixed signals, then no signals, and now he's acting interested again."

"He's always liked you as far as I know," she says, grabbing a drink from the table next to us. "You need to talk to him about it all, Corey. But for what it's worth, I'm rooting for you both. I always have been." She kisses me on the cheek and then goes to get her baby back.

"Yeah, I guess that's the mature thing to do," I mumble to myself, just as Jag comes up and gently nudges me.

"That's some talent you have," he compliments, clearly impressed. "I can't even draw a stick person that well."

I tilt my head to the side. "You're a tech genius and a hacker. You don't need to draw a stick anything."

Plus, by the look of him in his tight jeans, he wields a big enough stick.

He grins impishly, his green eyes alight with mischief. "True. And I have a decent body. And I'm pretty good-looking."

"Okay, calm down," I reply in a dry tone, but I can't help but laugh. Jag is always so light and fun to be around. "You're also clearly very modest."

"Name one modest biker," he states, scanning the crowd. "I don't know even one."

Now that he mentions it…

Okay, I suppose those two words don't really go well together.

"You know I like hanging out with you, right?" he says, flashing me a lopsided grin. "And you buy mangoes and chocolate, and you're cute as fuck. But even more than that, annoying Damon really is a

highlight for me. Look at him right now. He looks
like he wants to kill me."

I turn to look and see Damon talking with Jeremiah, having given Julian to Julianna, but his eyes
are locked on me, and he doesn't look happy at how
close Jag and I are standing and talking with each
other. I suppose I can see where Jag is coming from.
Maybe it will encourage Damon to carry me to my
bedroom, strip off my clothes, and show me firsthand
what all the fuss is about. And I know it's going to
be good, and well worth the wait, because just the
way he makes me feel from across the yard is intense
enough. I can only imagine what it will be like when
he's got me naked underneath him.

"You're drooling a little," Jag says, laughing as
he crosses his arms over his broad chest.

I wipe my mouth, which makes him laugh harder.

River comes over and stands next to me, an odd
expression on his face. "What's so funny?"

Is he worried something is happening with me and
Jag? Maybe it might make him appreciate Damon
more.

"Nothing," I reply in a sweet, singsong voice.
"What did you think of the mural?"

"I think it's perfect," he says, blue eyes gentling.
"Do you want me to take a photo of it so Mom can
see?"

The mention of my mother ruins my good mood.
"I don't think she'd really care, do you?"

The relationship I have with her is definitely a

sore point. I mean, who doesn't want a good relationship with their parents? They are the ones who
are supposed to show us unconditional love, and
instead I got saddled with an abusive father and a
mother who always treats me like she doesn't want
a daughter around. She clearly doesn't care—she's
off living her best life on River's money, fostering
animals instead of showing the same love and attention to her own child.

"I'm sure she'd love to see it. You got your artis-
tic side from her," he says, pulling out his phone and
going over to take the photo. He's so oblivious when
it comes to her.

Yeah, so maybe it'll get the attention of her narcis-
sistic side. She can claim my talent comes from her,
and then probably criticize it. Wonderful.

"He's such a proud brother," Jag points out, now
stretching his arms above his head with a yawn.
"And he doesn't look like he wants to kill me anymore whenever he sees me with you."

"Probably because he knows we're just friends
and you're usually just being a dickhead." I grin,
and Jag grabs me in a pretend headlock and messes
up my hair.

When I finally stand upright and gaze over at
Damon, he looks like he wants to kill us both.

"He's obviously not getting the friend zone
memo." Jag smirks, just as Leif, the Viking prospect, comes over to us, a beer in his hand.

"Your mural is amazing," he says, smiling. He's

tall, very, very tall, and his blond hair is loose around his shoulders.

"Thank you so much," I reply genuinely, just as River returns to show me the photo he took.

"Look how good it is, Corey. I'm sending it to her," he announces, pressing send.

"Want to send it to Tatum, too?" I joke, but then wish I didn't with the way his expression darkens.

"I don't know what game he's playing, but he's going to lose," he says, sliding his phone into his jeans pocket. "If he reaches out to you in any way, tell me right away. I wouldn't put it past him."

"I will. Don't worry, I have no foolish notions about wanting to get to know him," I say, crossing my arms over my chest. "As far as I'm concerned, I only have two brothers—one here and one in heaven."

"The third one is about to be in hell," I hear him mutter under his breath.

Damon finishes his conversation and strolls over to join the party, standing next to me. "Do you want something to drink?"

"Actually yes, I'd love a beer," I tell him, and he goes to get me one.

Good boy.

River watches him but doesn't say anything. I guess it's not a crime to be a gentleman.

"Who do you like better, Damon or Jag?" I ask, feeling a little bold this evening.

"Why?" he asks, lips tightening into a straight line. "You need to be more specific."

"Just in general," I insist, shrugging.

Something is going to happen with me and Damon. I can feel it in my bones, and I need to prepare River. But no matter how he reacts, I'm not going to let him control my life and tell me I can't be with who I want. That doesn't mean that I like him being upset, though.

"They're both my MC brothers" is all he says, giving nothing else away, but I know he has to like Damon more. Not that there's anything wrong with Jag, but he hasn't been around too long, with the Devils MC getting him in as a prospect a few months ago, and Damon has been an Angel for a long time, and is quickly moving up in the ranks.

River loves power, and he'd want me to be with someone like that. At least that's what I'm hoping.

The alcohol starts flowing, the music gets louder, and we all start having some fun as the sun goes down.

Once everyone is thoroughly inebriated, we ask Diamond if he can show us some of his stripper moves. We even put on "Pony" by Ginuwine. He does a little teasing body roll move, but then shakes his hands like *nope, sorry, not happening.*

But even that little move was sexy as hell.

"Come on!" we all cheer.

He laughs, a little nervously, rubbing the back of

his neck. "I'm sorry to disappoint, but I don't want to die before I'm patched in."

Smart man.

"Fair enough," Julianna replies, but low-key sounds disappointed.

"So where are all the single women?" he asks, taking a seat next to us. "Not that I don't enjoy your company, but I feel like daggers are being pointed at me every time I talk to one of you. And rightly so—you are all beautiful, and if you were mine, I wouldn't let you out of my sight, either."

I swallow hard, my mouth suddenly dry. "Well, we used to have more women around, but one of them ended up being a traitorous bitch, and we haven't really brought new women into the circle. But you're right, we should invite…" I pause. "All of our friends."

I share a look with Bella and Julianna, because we all know that we don't have any other friends.

There's Julianna's other sister, Veronica, who we're cool with, but she's kind of distanced herself ever since Julianna took over. She still lives with her parents, and Julianna does see her, but she doesn't really come to hang out. I mean, she was in love with Victor, who the MC did kill. There was also the woman who was supposed to work for Julianna and Bella and ended up being a spy for Rosalind.

Diamond reads the room. "You don't have any other friends, do you?"

We all burst out laughing, because it's true.

But we could find some, right?

When my phone buzzes with a text, I wonder who it could be because all of my friends are right here with me.

It's from an unknown number.

I'm not the monster everyone has made me out to be, Corey. And I AM your brother. Come meet me for a chat.

How the hell did he get my number?

Corey: Why are you here?

Tatum: I want to find out who killed my father. And we got kicked out of our last town, so I thought it was the perfect time. We can talk more in person.

Fuck.

Chapter Fifteen

Damon

The women keep laughing at Diamond, Mr. Magic Mike in the flesh, and suddenly I'm wondering why I gave him one of my votes.

"Whose idea was it bringing a stripper in here?" River scowls, downing the last of his drink. "I'm getting my woman and taking her to bed."

His departure means I get a little more freedom with Corey without starting a war, so I'm all over that. When she heads inside the clubhouse, I do the same, finding her in the kitchen halfway through packing away some of the food. She's looking at her phone, a concerned expression marring her brow.

"Are you okay?" I ask her, making her jump a little.

She turns to face me with her hand going to her chest. "You scared me, and look," she says, showing me her phone. "Tatum texted."

I read the message, my teeth clenching. "I'm glad you showed me. We need to tell Romeo."

"I know. Do you think Jag could trace his number from this?" she asks, resting her hip against the counter. "And how the hell did he even get my number?"

"I don't know."

She nods. "Yeah, I'll ask. Maybe we could use this to lure him out somewhere or something?"

Of course her mind would go there.

Corey would do anything for the people she loves, which means I need to worry about her putting herself in danger.

"You're not using yourself as bait," I reply, moving closer to her. She's so much smaller and shorter, she has to look up to see me.

"Why not?" she asks, putting her phone down on the table. "I know I messed up last time by trusting that snake Rosalind, but I'm not a weak woman."

I touch her cheek. "I have many words to describe you, Corey, and not one of them is *weak*."

She sighs and reaches her hand up to rest it on my chest. My heart stops. "I better finish packing this all away."

"You need some help?" I offer.

She smiles. "Yes, please. There's so much food left over. We are going to have to try to eat it all tomorrow."

We pack it all away until both the fridge and freezer are filled to the brim, and then I help her clean up the kitchen. We stand side by side, working in unison, me washing and her drying the dishes, without even having discussed it.

We seem to be a good team, and the thought fills me with resolve. I need to be honest with her and tell her how I'm feeling, and just hope that she still feels the same. That I'm not too late.

"We don't have any single women left at the clubhouse," she suddenly says, breaking the comfortable silence.

"Trust me, there are lots of single women around the men—we just don't invite them to family events," I say, smirking.

She pauses in her washing and turns angry hazel eyes to me. "Well, we all know you do. You brought Melinda to the clubhouse."

Here we go. But I'd rather the fire in her eyes than the flash of sadness when she called herself weak.

She is anything but.

She's the strongest woman I've ever met.

"I did not. She just showed up," I correct, wondering how the vibe changed so quickly. "And why even bring her up? She's not an issue anymore."

To be honest, I haven't even thought about her once, other than when Corey mentions her.

"I was just pointing out a fact," she replies, lifting her chin. She continues to wash and I continue to dry, although a little more aggressively this time.

Not everything has to turn into a fight, but I think with Corey I'm going to have to learn how to deal with her temper. I decide to stay quiet and see if that's the best way to calm her down without start-ing World War Three.

"Nothing to say?" she fires back.

"Not on that matter, no," I reply, our fingers touching when she hands me the plate. "But I do want to talk to you about us. Are we ready to stop playing around and actually explore what we have here? Because I know we have something. I knew it from the first time I saw you."

Her eyes widen as if she's surprised I'm finally putting it out there.

She clears her throat. "I'm ready. I've been ready, Damon. You're the one who has been playing games."

"Have you? Because after the kiss, you avoided me, too."

"I didn't want to start any trouble for you, I know how River can be," she admits, shifting on her feet. "But I didn't think you'd stop wanting me. I was waiting for you. Bikers take what they want, and you weren't taking me. Instead, you let me think you were dating Melinda for longer than you actu-ally were just to keep some distance between us!"

Fuck.

"I never once stopped wanting you. I'll never stop wanting you," I clear up.

She purses her lips. "Then why didn't you just fight for us?"

"I wanted to keep you safe! With everything going on with the club and me becoming sergeant at arms, I didn't want you caught in the crossfire. And then there's River, and of course the age thing was a bit of a concern for me," I admit, drying the last dish. "But you know what? So fucking what. I don't want anyone else, and life is too short for me to keep pretending otherwise. I can handle the club with you by my side, River will eventually get over it, and we're both adults."

I didn't want to jeopardize my growing role in the club.

But she's more important than even that.

I close the space between us and press my lips against hers. A gentle kiss. Sweet.

The opposite of what I'd like to do to her right now.

She pauses our kiss to look me in the eyes.

"Are you sure?" she asks. "You need to think about this because what you're saying changes everything, and I don't want you to change your mind and take it all back. I am ten years younger than you, and that's something you're going to have to accept."

We dry our hands, and then turn to face each other.

"I'm not going to take anything back," I promise her. "And I have accepted it. I don't want to change anything about you."

I offer her my hand.

She takes it.

We leave the kitchen, completely different people than when we stepped in.

She leads me to her new room, the tension between us heating up, and I catch her sneaking glances at me. Before she can open the door, I push her back against it and pin her hands. Her eyes stare into my soul with hazel fire, and I've never wanted anyone more.

"This is me taking what I want," I say, then kiss her deeply, the way I've been wanting to for so fucking long. She tastes so sweet, and her kiss has been well worth the wait.

When I pull back, she's breathless, and surprised, and has no usual smart-ass comeback.

Maybe this is the way to handle her.

She locks the door behind her. I don't know what she has planned, but I'm going to let her lead what happens tonight. I'm not going to have sex with her, though, because I want her first time to be a little more special, but that doesn't mean that I don't want to have a taste.

She tugs her top off, revealing a black bra, and then removes her shoes and jeans. I grin at her confidence, reaching behind me to pull my T-shirt off, throwing it on the floor with her belongings. She takes in my body, and then nods to my jeans. I hesitate, but then get rid of them too, leaving me in just my boxers. She laughs as I lift her up in my arms and carry her to the bed, our lips unable to leave each other.

It feels like a fucking dream to have her like this, and have her body pressed against mine.

I'm harder than I think I've ever been in my life, almost like it's my first time, too.

Which is crazy because I'm definitely not new to this. But experiencing it with her is making it feel that way.

I lay her back on her emerald-green bedsheets and kiss her slowly, trailing down her neck. Then I lift my head and memorize her face, her features, just taking her all in.

"Damon, I've been waiting a long time for this moment, don't you dare stop now," she growls, eyes narrowing.

I laugh softly. "We aren't going all the way tonight—"

"Damon!"

"It's your first time, it should be special—"

"You've finally decided to be with me. How is that not special?" she replies, rolling her eyes.

My lip twitches at the exasperation in her tone. "I didn't say I wasn't going to give you anything."

"What?" she asks, and then as I start kissing lower and lower until I reach the edge of her panties, she sighs. "Oh. Okay, that's very good."

I slide her panties down and spread her thighs. Pleasuring her and walking away after is going to be fucking hard, but tonight is all about her.

Chapter Sixteen

Corey

Lying back in the bed, my fingers in Damon's hair, I know that right now I'm not above begging. I might be coming off extremely horny and needy, but I've thought about this moment for so long, and now that it's here I'm fucking ready. I don't need to be sweet-talked, or for him to check in with me—he needs to just fuck me.

But I know that as it's my first time he wants to take it slow, and I appreciate that fact. He's being very sweet, and I have all the confidence that he's going to make this a memorable experience for me.

The first lick of his tongue on my clit is unlike anything I've felt. And then he really gets into it, and I'm so hot and turned on and wet and I'm trying to be quiet, but eventually I put a pillow over my face because I just want to scream in pleasure.

He slides his finger inside while still going down

on me, and it doesn't take long for me to come. My thighs tremble uncontrollably, and wave after wave of pleasure hits me from head to toe, sending shivers all over my body.

"Oh my god, orgasms are so much better when someone else does them," I blurt out, and he starts laughing with his mouth still on me.

Especially when it's someone that you have wanted for so damn long.

And just when I think it's over, he goes again, slowly working me up for another orgasm. But this time he flips me over onto my stomach and lifts my hips, spreading my thighs and putting his mouth on my sex from behind. I hold on to the headboard while he devours me. I could get used to this.

I come another two more times, and then I push him off me, lying back and catching my breath.

When I expect him to fuck me next, he doesn't. Instead, he lies down next to me, and I can see how hard his cock is, but he doesn't seem to be wanting to do anything with it. So I take charge and pull it out of his boxer shorts.

And wow.

It's big.

Huge.

"Damon, this thing is a monster," I say, and he starts laughing, his cock shaking with the motion.

Until I start stroking him. Then the laughter stops and the moaning starts.

I lick my hand to get it nice and wet and work my magic.

What I lack in experience, I'm making up for in enthusiasm.

"Fuck, Corey," he grits out, and hearing my name on his lips is such a turn-on.

And his raspy moans are so sexy.

And then he comes, and I am absolutely mesmerized. The wild, heated look in his eyes, the way his teeth bite into his full lower lip.

It was the hottest thing I've ever seen, and I can understand now why he's so happy to give so much without taking. I could watch him lose all control like that forever.

"Can we do that again?" I ask on a breathless whisper.

He shakes his head at me, flashes me a panty-dropping grin and rolls me back over.

Now this is what I'm talking about.

When I wake up, he's gone, and for a second I wonder if it was all a dream.

Did I drink too much last night?

But then I see a text from him on my phone.

Damon: Was hard to leave you this morning but had to get out of there before your brother murdered me. Need to talk to him today. Miss you already. I told Romeo about the text from Tatum.

Corey: Miss you too. I had fun last night. Seconds tonight?

Apparently, I'm a very single-minded woman.

Damon: I'm not just a piece of meat.

Laughing, I type back.

Corey: Aw, come on. I'll buy you dinner first at least.

Damon: Very funny.

Bella: Lunch today? What are your plans?

Lunch sounds amazing, but before I tell her that I type back to Damon first.

Corey: I can't help it, your cock is just so big and delicious.

I then reply to Bella, but when I go to type in the message, I realize that I just sent the last text to Bella and not Damon.

Oh.

My.

God.

I try to unsend it, but it's too late. The little tick lets me know that she's already seen it.

I will never look Bella in the eyes again. I'm going to die of embarrassment.

Rolling over, I hide my face in my pillow, and scream.

Why me?

When my phone buzzes, it takes me a whole twenty minutes before I have the guts to read it.

Bella: I'm guessing that text wasn't for me. LOL.

Bella: Oh my god, did you see Damon's penis last night? Is he there now?

Fucking hell.

I resend the same message to Damon and tell him I accidentally sent it to Bella, then get out of bed and into the shower.

He has replied by the time I get out.

Damon: You sent that to Bella? HAHAHAHAHA.

Damon: But also, tell me more.

Bella: Don't ignore me.

Although I'd like to, I can't ignore her forever, so I bite the bullet and reply.

Corey: Can we pretend that text never happened please? Like let's never mention it again. And yes, let's have lunch. Do not tell River anything. Damon will talk to him when he's ready.

I love my brother, but he doesn't control my life. I understand him wanting to protect me, but I'm almost twenty now, and it's time for me to experience things, and fall in love and be free.

He has Bella, and he can't expect me to be alone forever, just because he feels like no one is good enough for me. Don't get me wrong, I appreciate the sentiment, and it has encouraged me to set a high standard with men and for myself, but Damon is more than good enough.

He's perfect for me.

And I'd like to explore that without River starting fights and carrying on.

I get ready and head out to lunch with Bella, feeling awkward as fuck, but there's nothing much I can do. At least it was her and not my brother, because then I'd have to move countries.

"Hello," she says when I walk up to the table, big smile on her face. I can feel the heat on my cheeks, and I just know I'm blushing like a fucking tomato right now. "Good night?"

"Something like that," I murmur, fiddling with the hem of my denim dress as I sit down. "I'm here to debrief with you, but I don't want to hear any shit, you got it?"

She nods, trying to hide her grin and failing miserably. "So… Damon. Big D…"

"I'm going to kill you," I say, covering my face with my hands. "But yes. It was huge. Not that I have much to compare it with, but it was basically the size of my arm."

I lower my hand and look into her beautiful eyes.

She looks happy.

For me.

"Tell me everything, no detail is too small."

"Well, we didn't have sex. He didn't want to since we only just decided we liked each other yesterday," I explain, smiling to myself. "But we did... other things, and yes. He was very generous, and good, so good."

With everything.

His hands, his mouth, his tongue.

Perfection.

"I'm so excited for you, and I'm so glad Damon finally realized what he had right in front of him," she says, doing a little happy dance, wriggling on the chair.

"I wonder how River is going to take it," I say, wrapping my arms around myself. I hate fighting with him. But this is a hill I'll die on.

"I'll handle River," she assures me, reaching out and touching my hand. "You aren't his little baby anymore, and he needs to accept that."

"I don't want you to argue with him over me," I reply, feeling bad.

She waves away my concern. "We aren't going to get into a fight. I will just gently tell him that you are not doing anything wrong, and neither is Damon. Love is a blessing."

"Okay, thank you."

It's good to know that she will have my back if it all goes south.

But let's just all hope it doesn't come to that.

Jag shows up and joins us, because apparently we aren't supposed to be going anywhere alone, and we all have lunch together and then head back.

In the car I stare at the text from Tatum and wonder if I could get some information out of him if I replied. I haven't spoken to Romeo or River about it, and I know they'd kill me if I just texted him back without letting them know.

But I'm tempted.

Corey: What do you want to talk about?

Shit.

Chapter Seventeen

Damon

I'm working at Devil's Play tonight, a burlesque dance club that the Devils MC started and own. Since we've joined our motorcycle clubs, and Romeo's trust in me has grown, he's been letting me handle things more and more, and tonight, I'm the one on call for any issues that may arise at the club.

Jag: Lost Lions MC members spotted in the area.

Damon: You think they'll come here?

Jag: Maybe.

I need to be prepared, in case. This venue is always packed, attracting a big crowd. I'm happy to be here, but I'd rather be back at the clubhouse with Corey, who I now might not be able to see tonight.

Echo, the manager, walks by me with her clipboard in hand. I remember once when I was asking about Corey, Bella tried to talk me into being interested in Echo instead, telling me she's another redhaired beauty.

And she is, don't get me wrong, but she's not for me.

There's no other woman who makes me feel the spark that Corey does.

Sometimes the penis wants what the penis wants, or whatever that saying is.

I send Corey a text letting her know I probably won't be able to see her tonight. It's too risky dropping into the Devils clubhouse at nighttime anyway. If River sees me, he will definitely know something is up, and he will lose his shit.

And fighting with him puts me in a lose/lose situation, because at the end of the day he is Corey's only family left, and she loves him like crazy.

If I kick his ass, I would be the bad guy.

If I don't and kiss his ass, I'll look weak to the club.

He's also a psychopath, and the enforcer for the club, so he basically has a degree in torture and murder.

So he's not really someone I want to fight with.

That doesn't mean that I'd back down, though.

I'm a good fighter, and well trained at that, and I know how to defend myself.

Name one biker who doesn't.

I nod. "Yep. Is there anything you'd like me to do?"

She gives me a once-over, and my eyes widen in surprise. Echo doesn't hit on any of the men in the MC. In fact, I was starting to think she might be into women, because the men told me that they've never seen her even as so much show interest in the opposite sex.

But I know that look.

"I mean, what are you doing after this?" she asks, looking me right in the eye. She's confident, and bold. And straight to the point.

"Oh, um." I move closer to her. "I'm kind of seeing someone."

She sighs and crosses her arms. "Of course you are. The first and only time I make a move on a man, and you're suddenly seeing someone."

I grin and lean over the bar. "Echo, I'm flattered, and you are a gorgeous woman. I'm sure no single man would turn down you down. But yes, I'm seeing someone new, and… I'm fucking crazy about her."

"So that's why you're so distracted," she comments, arching her brow, her green eyes knowing. "I'm sorry, I shouldn't have… That was out of character for me. And extremely unprofessional."

"Don't worry about it, it never happened," I say, flashing her a smile. "You should come hang out at the clubhouse some time. The women were saying they don't have any friends."

She tilts her head to the side, mulling it over. "If

I'm hoping we can just talk it out, and deal with it in a civilized way. We both respect each other, so why not?

"Damon," Echo calls, placing her clipboard on the bar and studying me. "Are you okay? You seem distracted."

"I'm fine," I say, smiling at a group of people that enters, scanning them to see if I recognize anyone. Lions members specifically. Echo takes their money and leads them into the club.

Corey: Wait, you're where? At the strip club?

Shit.

Damon: It's a burlesque club, and you know that. And I'm working, Romeo wanted me here in case anything goes wrong. We're short one security guard.

She doesn't reply.

Fucking hell.

An hour passes, and still no response.

Is she already mad at me? That has to be some kind of record.

I wander outside and stand with the security checking ID at the door, and then do a perimeter check. The loud music hits me when I head back inside, and Echo looks up from the bar at the entrance. "Everything okay?"

I'm being honest, I don't have any, either. It's just been work and home for me."

"Well, there you go. I'll let them know."

She looks over my head at the door. "I think you can tell them yourself."

"What?" I reply, following her line of sight.

Shit.

Corey, Bella, and Julianna step through the door. They never come here.

Okay, this can't be good, and I'm the only one here so I'm going to have to deal with them all. Not only that—it's really not safe right now for them to be traipsing all over the fucking town alone.

Corey's eyes are on Echo, and she's looking at her like she wants to tear her throat out.

"Ladies, what a lovely surprise," I say, then turn to Corey, giving her a slow perusal. "Corey, you look amazing."

She's in a silky dress I'd like to rip off with my teeth later, and her hair is half up, half down. She doesn't reply to my compliment, instead stepping closer and lowering her voice. "We just wanted to come out and have a drink. We aren't disturbing you both, are we?"

Shit.

"No, of course not. Do you want a table in there?" I ask, looking at them all. "And what did you want to drink?"

"We'd love a table," Julianna replies, looking at the other two. "Spicy margaritas?"

"Sounds good," Bella replies, and Corey nods.

"I'll get the table and drinks," Echo says, disappearing into the club's main room.

"Where are Romeo and River tonight?" I ask. Not watching their women, I can tell you that much.

Julianna smirks, then glances around the lobby. "Not at home to stop us from coming here."

Wonderful.

"I've always wanted to come," Bella says, linking her arm with Corey's. "And when Corey suggested we do, I jumped at it."

Echo comes back out, the music getting louder as she opens the door. "Table is ready for you."

They walk past me, and I grab Corey's arm as she does. "I'm here working—nothing else is going on."

"Would you like it if I worked around hot, half-naked men?" she whisper-yells back at me. "You didn't even like Diamond *talking* to us about his stripping."

I don't know how Diamond is getting brought into this.

"Of course I wouldn't like it, but Corey, all of the men come work here at one point or another. We do what Romeo or Julianna tell us to do," I try to explain to her. "And you know I'm being given more responsibility in the club now. And I'm not even in there watching the show, I'm here making sure there are no security problems. You know, just in case your *other* brother and his men suddenly show up here."

"Yeah, instead you're alone here leaning over the

table talking to the hot older redhead," she replies in a dry tone, putting her hands on her hips. "This is my fault for choosing a man who is so incredibly good-looking."

She walks inside, and I grin at the compliment.

If only she knew that she has nothing to worry about.

I'm going to make it my mission to make sure that she does.

Chapter Eighteen

Corey

I came here tonight with a lot of jealousy, and pettiness…but I'm actually having such a good time. The cocktails are flowing, the show is actually really good, and the dancers are so talented. I find myself admiring their sexy costumes, the fishnet stocking and feather boas, and their seductive dance moves.

I might have overreacted a little by making the women come here tonight just so I could see with my own eyes what Damon was up to. I can now see that I'm definitely showing my crazy a little too soon, especially when he was open with how my age was a concern for him.

I'm not coming off as the most mature.

I shouldn't have come in here tonight, guns blazing, when he was working.

But now that I'm here, it's actually turned into

such a fun girls' night, and I've mostly forgotten that Damon is even here.

"We need to do this more often," Bella says, lifting her glass up. "Cheers to us, letting loose. Thank you, Corey, for being crazy enough about Damon to make us show up here."

Truth be told, they didn't want to come and tried to talk me out of it. But Julianna didn't put her foot down, which she easily could have, so maybe she wanted a night out, too, letting her parents keep Julian for the first time. I know that we aren't supposed to be out without the men with us because of everything going on with Tatum and his MC, but Damon is here, so that counts for something, right?

There's no way he hasn't messaged Romeo and River and told them where their women are.

I excuse myself and get up and go to the bathroom, where I find Echo looking at herself in the mirror.

"Hey," I say, and she smiles and wipes her eyes. Was she crying? "Is everything okay?"

"Yeah, everything is fine," she replies, clearing her throat. "So Damon tells me you guys were maybe looking for some new friends."

I laugh, feeling tipsy after my three drinks. Although technically I'm not legal yet, it's never been an issue for any establishment owned by the MC. "Yeah, I did say that. We realized we didn't have anyone else that we actually liked."

She smiles sadly and straightens the collar of

her blouse, and it hits me that maybe she needs a friend, too.

"Are you finished with work?"

"Yeah, I'm done for the night."

"Would you like to join us for a drink?" I ask.

It's not her fault that she's gorgeous and a way more sophisticated and sexy redhead than I am. She looks sad, and a little vulnerable, and I think she needs someone to reach out to her. I've heard only good things about Echo from all the men, and how professional she is.

"Really?" she asks, sounding surprised. "I don't want to interrupt your night…"

I wave my hand in the air. "The more the merrier. I only came here because I wanted to see where Damon was spending his night, and just how close he was getting to the dancers."

Green eyes widen. "Oh, you and Damon?"

"It's new," I admit, wincing. I probably shouldn't tell everyone yet. For all we know next week we could be back to ignoring each other. "But don't repeat that, please."

"Of course," she replies, hiding her grin.

She heads out while I use the restroom and check my texts, but there's no reply from Tatum. I'm well aware River and Damon would be pissed to know what I am doing, but I find myself falling deeper into it anyway.

When I get back to the table, Echo is sitting there, and Julianna and Bella are ordering her a drink.

"Thanks so much," she says to all of us. "I've had the worst day, and some company right now is just what I need."

"Of course," Bella says. "We know you've worked for the MC for so long, but we've never really hung out with you without the men."

"I've tried to keep everything strictly business with the MC, so I usually keep my distance," Echo admits, taking a long sip of her drink. "But now I can see that I've isolated myself by doing that."

I feel for Echo and the spot she's in.

And if I'm being honest, when I walked in and saw her talking with Damon so closely, I did feel jealous. But she works alongside them, and she's never slept with any of them, so she's never stepped on any toes.

Something must have happened and maybe she's realized that she doesn't want to be so alone anymore. I think that everyone can relate to that in some stage of their life. I know I can. I've always considered myself a lone wolf, but I love the people I have around me, and I'd never want to be without them.

At the end of the show, we are all cheering and tipping the dancers.

Damon comes and sits with us at the end, bringing us another round of drinks.

"This was fun," I tell them all, my head buzzing in the very best way. "I've had the best night, so thank you."

Romeo and River show up, looking less than impressed.

"Hey, husband," Julianna says to Romeo, sliding up to him. "I know, I know. Save the lecture. Damon was here and we were safe. Now let's go home."

Romeo kisses her and whispers something into her ear. Her cheeks warm and she clears her throat.

Romeo then looks over at me. "We need to talk about those text messages."

"What messages?" Julianna asks, arching her brow.

"Tatum contacted her," he explains, and I shrug.

Julianna widens her eyes. "Saying what? Did he threaten you?" she asks as she grabs my arm.

A fierceness enters her eyes, and I see the President of the Angels MC in her come out. She really was born to rule.

"No, he didn't threaten me. He wanted me to meet him, though," I admit.

Julianna loosens her grip on my arm. "I'm glad you didn't. You need to be careful with Tatum. He's unpredictable. You can't put yourself in any danger." She pulls me in for a hug. "I don't know what I would do if anything happened to you."

River comes over and Bella says something to him quietly. Then he turns to me and narrows his eyes. "Come on, Corey. We're all going home."

Damon walks over and stands next to me, and River looks between the two of us.

Shit.

Bella takes my arm and leads me away, leaving the two men alone together.

I knew this was going to have to happen, but now that it's here, I'm terrified. Luckily the alcohol takes the edge off.

I just hope that River doesn't decide to be an asshole and say that he doesn't approve of Damon.

"What do you think they're saying?" I ask Bella, trying to look around her and lip-read. "Do you think River is going to be reasonable?"

"I spoke to him, don't worry," she assures me, pulling me to the bar. "Let's have another drink. You can't control what happens next, so don't stress out about it. Either way, in the end, it will be fine."

"You're right." I nod and take her offer on the drink. "How about a shot?"

"I'm going to suffer tomorrow, but sure," she replies, and slides me a menu. "How about tequila?"

Sounds like regret. "Let's do it."

"You're going to endanger her even more!" I hear River yell at Damon.

Endanger me? Because he's moving up in the club? River is my fucking brother—I've already got a target on my back anyway.

I've got the lime in my mouth when I turn around and see River punch Damon right in the jaw. Damon takes it and doesn't retaliate.

I get off the barstool and try to go to them, but Bella grabs me by my arm and holds me back. "Let them handle it."

"He hit him!" I say, trying to get her hands off me. "I'm going to kill him!"

Damon has done nothing wrong! And my own brother shouldn't be angry that someone is finally making me happy and loving me the way that I deserve.

River is not going to ruin this for me, even if he's coming from a good place. I'm not a child anymore.

Bella gives up and lets me go. I rush to my brother to give him an earful. "River, I love him, and I don't care what you have to say. Do you hear me? And don't ever put your hands on him again, or I'm going to…"

I trail off when I see Damon's expression, filled with amusement, pride, and pure fucking happiness. His eyes gentle as he gives me a long, searching look.

"What?" I whisper-yell at him.

Did I just blurt out that I loved him?

Yes, yes I did.

"You can calm down, Corey," River says, looking me in the eye. "I don't love it, but as Bella pointed out to me, I probably wouldn't like anyone. Damon is a good man, and an Angel moving up in the club, and I suppose it could be worse. But if he hurts you, I'm going to skin him alive and enjoy every second of it."

I open my mouth, only to close it and open it again. "Then why did you hit him?"

"I asked him if he'd spent the night with you yet. He said he had. That's what he gets. You both should have had this conversation with me before then,"

River says with a blank face. His arms cross over his chest.

"That is none of your business, though! But if you must know, we didn't even have sex!" I point out, my hands clenching to fists.

He is one nosy motherfucker.

He winces and shakes his head. "Yeah, I don't need the details, baby sister. I love you, but you're right. You are an adult now, and I can't keep you locked away forever. But I just wanted to warn him what's coming if he ever hurts you."

Wait, what?

"No, you can't," I murmur, studying him carefully. Is he really not being overprotective and controlling? "And what happens is between me and Damon—it has nothing to do with you."

A muscle works in his jaw, but he nods.

It's a Christmas fucking miracle. I jump on him and hug him, catching him off guard. He grunts as he takes my sudden impact. "Thank you, River. I love you, you know that, right?"

"I do, and the feeling is mutual," he says, squeezing me back. "Now let's get home—you shouldn't have dragged everyone out here tonight without letting us know in the first place."

"How did you know it was me?" I ask with a frown, wondering who snitched.

He arches his brow, but says nothing, instead heading over to Bella and pulling her out of there.

I turn to Damon, who is watching me intensely.

"What?" I ask, a slow smile taking over.

"You said that you loved me," he replies, cupping my face and scanning my eyes. He tucks my hair back behind my ear, his eyes filled with something that sends tingles all over my body.

Shit.

"I'm tipsy—don't listen to anything that I say right now," I blurt out, but we both know the truth.

I did mean it, and I think I've loved him for a long time now.

But he doesn't need to know all my secrets, and drunk me needs to shut up and keep her thoughts to herself.

He simply laughs and kisses me. "You love me," he whispers against my lips.

I rest my forehead against his and nod.

Yeah, I fucking love him.

We share another sweet, gentle kiss filled with emotion.

He takes me back to the clubhouse, to his bedroom, to stay the night.

No River.

No hiding.

Just him, and me.

Finally.

Chapter Nineteen

Damon

I leave my motorcycle at the club and take Corey home in the car, because she's had one too many drinks to sit on the back safely. I've never brought a woman back to the clubhouse, mostly because I never wanted anyone in my business, but also because it always felt too personal to have them in my space, surrounded by my family. But with Corey it feels so natural.

"I just wanted to say that I should have told you I was going to come out tonight," she says, staring at my profile as I drive. "I mean, it was a last-minute decision after you told me you were there, but still. Thinking of you being around sexy women dancing made me extremely jealous, and I was impulsive."

"You can trust me, Corey. If I wanted to fuck around with dancers, I could have been doing that this whole time. I only want you," I assure her, reaching out and touching her thigh. "No one else."

"Okay." She nods, resting her hand on my own. "Then I will trust you until you give me a reason not to. Tonight ended up being the best night ever, though. River accepted us and let me leave with you, and I had an amazing time with the girls. And I even made a new friend in Echo. I think she really needed some friends tonight, and I'm glad she came and hung out with us. She gave me her number, so next time we do something I can invite her."

"I'm sure she'd love that," I reply, smiling at her excited tone. One thing I'm not going to do is tell her that Echo did kind of hit on me tonight, because I don't need to ruin their friendship before it begins.

"Where are we going?" she asks, when I don't turn down the road leading to the clubhouse, taking a last-minute detour.

"I'm going to get you something to eat—and something to drink," I tell her, parking the car at the service station. I lean over to her, kiss her, and then say against her lips, "Because the first time I'm going to have you, you aren't going to be drunk."

"Trust me, I'm suddenly feeling very sober," she replies, teeth sinking into her lower lip.

I grin and get out of the car to buy some water, soda, painkillers, and snacks in case she has a hangover tomorrow.

"Let's stop and get you something to eat," I say to her when I slide back in.

"I'd love a burger," she replies, so I head back the other way and stop to get her whatever she wants. "And then I'd love you to take me home and fuck me. Finally."

I almost choke on my sip of water.

"I'm so ready, Damon, you have no idea. And the fact that it's you that's going to be my first makes me so fucking ready," she sighs. "And I'm not drunk anymore, so don't even try to use that as an excuse."

Fuck.

I shift in my seat, my cock hardening. "If you want food, you'd better stay quiet, or I'm going to take you straight home and fuck you."

She seems to consider my words, and then reaches over and strokes my thigh, and then my cock, a hiss escaping me at the contact over my jeans.

"Corey," I warn.

"Fuck the food," she whispers.

I turn the car around.

The ride back is tense, especially with her teasing, and I'm so fucking hard that I'm going to burst the second she touches me.

When we get inside, I lead her to my bedroom and lock the door behind us. She sits down on my bed and looks around my room, and then starts unbuckling the straps of her heels. I kneel and help her, and then look up to see her beautiful hazel eyes on me, a happy expression etched onto her face.

"You look good on your knees," she says, lip twitching.

Fuck, she's going to be the death of me.

"Corey—"

"Are you going to help me take the rest off?" she asks, and I grin and get her out of her tight black dress, bra, and panties.

She squeals a little when I pick her up, grabbing the bare globes of her ass and moaning at the handful. "God, look at you. Perfect."

"Should we have a quick shower?" she asks, and I carry her into the bathroom, turning on the hot water. She jumps in while I strip down and get in there with her. She's tied her hair on top of her head in a messy bun, a few loose curly strands falling on her face. I brush them back and try to hide my expression as she takes me in from head to toe, running her fingers down my abs.

"How is this all mine?" she asks, looking down at my cock with wide eyes. "It's…a very nice size."

Shit.

If she keeps talking to it like that, it's going to get a whole lot bigger.

We rub soap on each other, and her casual touches and strokes turn me on so much. I can't wait to be inside of her, but I want to make it a good experience for her and take it slowly, no matter how ready she says she is. She makes it hard when she reaches out to stroke me, and I pick her up and kiss her, pushing her back against the glass screen. She wraps her legs around me and her arms hold onto my neck. Her wet, beautiful body pressed against mine snaps even my strong will, and I turn the water off, dry us both off, and take her to bed.

After I put on a slow jam playlist and grab a condom out of my top drawer, I get under the sheets next to her, and she doesn't hesitate.

She pulls me to her and kisses me deeply, her intention clear.

She's ready, and she wants me now.

I roll her onto her back and take my time teasing her, and then go down on her and make her come with my tongue. Now that I'm learning what she likes, she finishes a lot faster this time, and then I slide the protection on and rub my cock against her pussy.

"Are you sure?" I ask her, but she cuts me off before I can barely get the sentence out.

"Yes, Damon. Fuck me, please," she begs, and so I start to slide in slowly, sucking and licking her nipples while I do so. I bite down gently, and she seems to like that, so I do it again as I push my hard cock all the way in.

I lift my head to check on her, and what a fucking sight it is. Her cheeks are flushed, her lips are parted, and her eyes are filled with lust.

She lifts her hips against me, impatient, so I give her what she wants, still holding myself back so that I don't hurt her.

"Hard. I want it hard," she whispers in my ear, digging her nails into my back.

And so, I let loose, and show her the side of me she's been longing to know.

I make her mine.

Chapter Twenty

Corey

When the sunlight streams into the bedroom, I stretch my arms over my head and smile wider than ever.

I'm finally not a virgin anymore.

And how fucking glorious the night was.

Damon made me feel so sexy, so cared for, and so hot and satisfied, and I now know why people make such a big deal about sex.

It's everything.

I could happily stay in this bedroom for the next month, just fucking him over and over again. It's like he can read my mind, but really, it's just him listening to my body and giving it what it needs, and once I gave him permission to do so, his animalistic side really took over and just…wow.

"Good morning," he says in a husky tone when he rolls over and notices I'm awake. "I was going to get up and make you some breakfast in bed."

"I'm not going to say no," I reply, kissing him.

"How do you feel?" he asks with a smile, getting up.

"Wonderful," I say, staring at his naked body and feeling that stir once more. I could go again, right now.

He turns around at my tone, eyes darkening. "Corey…"

"Yes?"

"Why are you looking at me like that? I know you have to be sore today," he says, sliding on a pair of boxer shorts.

But he's hard.

No one can miss that.

"You better not be walking out like that," I tell him, sitting up against the pillows and pulling the sheet with me. "And I'm a little sore, but it's fine. It's a good kind of sore."

He leans down to kiss me. "I'll be back with food."

"I'll be here waiting."

When he disappears from the room I get up and have a quick shower and brush my teeth. I don't have any fresh clothes to wear so I just put on one of his T-shirts, but I'm going to have to wear my dress back home in a walk of shame that everyone is going to know about. The thought of walking in and having River see me before I've changed makes me feel sick. Maybe I should just move out and get my own place now, so I don't have to deal with these unnecessary awkward moments. The thought reminds me how far I've come. I used to hate leaving the club-house and my anxiety taking over, but now? I feel a lot more confident.

Damon soon returns with toast, bacon, eggs, and coffee.

"Thank you," I say, and I notice him eying my clothing as I take the plate from him. I pointedly ignore my phone in case Tatum has messaged me again. "I hope you don't mind—I didn't want to put my tight dress back on."

"I don't mind at all," he responds, tone husky. "You eat. I'm going to jump in the shower."

He disappears and I've eaten about half the food when he comes out in nothing but a towel on his hips. His body is incredible, and I'm just lucky he didn't choose to become a stripper like Diamond, because he'd make a killing. I never thought I'd be so into abs, but I can't take my eyes off them, and last night I had my tongue running through every ripped line.

I put the plate down on the bedside table and continue to watch him, a different hunger taking over. He's appeased one, and now the other has come back to play.

"You know, there's one thing we haven't done yet that I've been thinking about."

"And what's that?" he asks, arching his brow in amusement. I get up and run my palms over his smooth chest, and place a kiss in the center. Slowly, I kiss downward, flicking his towel so it drops to the floor, and then get on my knees.

"Fuck, you look so beautiful on your knees," he rasps, swallowing hard at the sight of me.

I grin.

I've wanted to go down on him ever since he did it to me, but I suppose I was a little unsure at the start. Since then, I've grown more confident, and I've also done a quick internet search on how to do it well enough that it will blow his mind and make him think I'm the best he's ever had. Not that it's a competition.

But, well, I want to be the best.

Okay, it's totally a competition.

I know, I'm toxic, sue me.

Just like I read online, I take his big, thick cock in my hands and look up with him, using the doe eyes I've been practicing. I've gotten pretty good at this—you may as well call me fucking Bambi.

Then I put the head into my mouth and suck, before taking as much of it in as I can, getting it nice and wet. Going by the look on his face he's having a good time, and his penis is so hard, it looks like it's throbbing and pointing at me violently.

"Fuck," he groans.

I keep sucking, licking, and swallowing as much as I can, my hands working the base in a twisting motion that I hope I'm doing right. I should have watched a proper instruction video instead of reading about it. His hands gently thread through my hair and he starts making these deep growly sounds that make me relax into the moment and stop thinking so much. I just give it all I have, and I start to enjoy it too.

And then he tries to push me off. "I'm going to come."

Perfect.

The words *finish him* blast through my head like that video game, which make me smirk around him.

I keep the same pressure and strokes up, just like I read, and soon enough he finishes in my mouth. I was planning on spitting it out, but last minute it seems easier to just swallow and not think about it. I drain every drop out of him, sucking gently even when he's done, sending his body trembling.

"Holy fuck, Corey," he pants out, grabbing me and laying me back on the bed next to him. "That was so hot."

I smile.

Mission accomplished.

And then he rolls over and spreads my thighs, returning the favor.

And I'm in my new happy place.

Chapter Twenty-One

Damon

Corey borrows some of Bella's clothes, since we're all in the process of merging into the new clubhouse, before heading back to the Devils clubhouse. Last night was a long time coming, and it was totally worth the wait. I feel so much closer to her now, and to be honest I don't want her to leave.

"You should move in with me here," I tell her, changing gears. "Soon everyone will be moving here anyway, so why not just do it now?"

Her eyes widen, surprised. "I mean, I can go back and forth without officially *moving*. I know you have moved in here, but the renovations aren't even all done yet."

"It has everything we need," I say, eying her. "Or at least it will if you're here."

She smiles and reaches out to touch my arm. "We'll work it out."

I think the head she gave me this morning has my brain all fucked up. I almost wanted to ask her if she's sure she hasn't done it before, because she definitely knew her way around my dick. I tried to last as long as I could, but her mouth was like a fucking vacuum and before I knew it, I was filling her up. I thought she'd pull away, but nope, she swallowed every fucking drop.

I'm getting hard again just thinking about it.

"That sounds reasonable," I reply with a smirk because I'm glad she's thinking straight. I just want her with me.

Twenty-four motherfucking seven.

But she's right, we've come this far and now there's no rush. I'm just thinking about what we shared and greedily wanting her again.

Focus, Damon.

"I'm glad that you had a good time, though," she replies, amusement etched all over her face. "Because I know I sure as hell did. I'd like to be locked away with you for days on end..."

"Are you going to come back over tonight, then?" I ask, tone low and deep. "Because I have a few more ideas..."

"I don't see why not," she replies.

I get out of the car and walk her inside, where River happens to be sitting on the couch, facing the door, likely waiting for his sister to get home.

"Good morning," she says to him, leaning on the doorframe. "What are you doing?"

"Nothing," he replies, clearing his throat. "Just about to head out for a ride. How about you?"

I hide my smirk at him not wanting to admit to her that he's been sitting here waiting to make sure she gets home safe. Poor man probably didn't get any sleep.

That makes three of us.

Bella comes out with coffee and smiles warmly at the two of us. "You're back, alive and well, thank goodness. Now we can get on with our day."

"Of course I'm alive and well," Corey replies, pursing her lips. "Are we still having dinner tonight?"

"Yes, I made the booking. Did you want to join us, Damon?" Bella asks, sitting down next to River.

"I'd love to, but Romeo wants me back at Devil's Play tonight," I say, looking at Corey as I realize I forgot to tell her that. "He'll probably want me there all this week until we get enough security back in place. I think a couple of the prospects will be joining me, too."

"Yeah, Diamond and Leif," River confirms. I can tell he doesn't love me being with his sister, or the fact that she stayed at my house last night. But he's containing himself, and I think that has a lot to do with Bella's influence. It's great that he's accepting the fact that Corey is a grown woman, and maybe he realized that being with a member of the MC is a best-case scenario.

Better the devil you know, right?

Or an angel in this case.

I kiss Corey goodbye and get out of there, telling her I will pick her up on my way home from the club if she'd like to stay the night. At least she doesn't seem fazed about me going back to Devil's Play, which is a relief because it would suck if that became a thing.

I spend the rest of the day working with some of the men to lay out some of the security plans of the new clubhouse and then trying to figure out what is going on at the storage unit with the Lions. They still keep going but I don't have any idea. I've even taken to renting my own storage unit to gain access, but nothing.

After meeting Julianna to finalize plans on moving everyone into the joint clubhouse, and running some errands for Romeo, I head home to have some dinner and get ready for another night at Devil's Play.

Echo is speaking to a few of the dancers when I walk in, with everyone getting ready for tonight's show.

"Hey," she says when she sees me. "Diamond and Leif are helping move chairs and tables."

"Good," I reply with a smirk. "Get them to do whatever you need. We'll be here for a couple of hours to help out."

"Thanks," she replies, glancing down at her clipboard and back up. "I just wanted to apologize again for last night. I had no idea you and Corey were a thing, and if I had, I never would have propositioned you. She's absolutely beautiful, and I'd never do that to another woman. So, I'm sorry."

"No apology needed, Echo. I know the person you are," I reply, gently touching her shoulder. "Seriously, forget about it. And I'm happy that you and the girls hung out and had a good time."

"We really did," she says, smiling at a dancer who walks by. "I just haven't been myself these last few days. Maybe I'm having a midlife crisis or something. I don't know."

I pull out a barstool and sit down. "No judgment here. But at the end of the day, you are human. So be kind to yourself. You can't be an emotionless workaholic all of your life."

Her jaw drops open. "Is that how you see me? Wonderful. No wonder I haven't had sex in years. Years, Damon."

Diamond walks out just time to hear the last part. "Years? Why? You're smoking hot."

She turns to him, clearing her throat. "Well, thank you. But I think I come off as a cold bitch, so that's probably why."

"Maybe it's because you work for bikers," he suggests, giving her a once-over. "No one would want to deal with that. You don't seem cold at all. I imagine you'd warm up with the right touch."

I slowly back away from their conversation and head back to the office to make sure all the security cameras are in working order. My phone buzzes with a text.

Corey: I miss you.

Damon: I miss you, too. How's dinner?

Corey: Good. River is on his best behavior. I don't know what Bella said to him, but it's worked.

Damon: That's good. I'll text you when I'm on the way to pick you up.

Corey: I can meet you there if it's easier?

Damon: No, I'll get you. It's not safe.

Better to be safe than sorry. I don't want her going anywhere alone, and especially not at night.

And Corey has only just become mine, and now she's mine to protect.

And I take that job very seriously.

I'm not taking any chances.

And then it happens.

The members of the Lost Lions MC show up at the Devil's Play doors, showing up like they fucking belong here.

I tell Echo to call Romeo, and step outside with security to stop them.

Chapter Twenty-Two

Corey

"What did you say to River to make him okay with everything? He hasn't made a snide comment all night," I ask Bella when River gets up to pay the bill.

"I just told him that you're a grown woman, and he's holding you back by not letting you experience life. And it might push you away," she explains, lifting her wineglass to her lips and taking a sip. "He loves you so much, Corey. But he can love you and let you live your life, too. So that's what he's doing."

"I don't know what I'd do without you."

She laughs and leans toward me. "You'd probably have died a virgin."

"You're right," I deadpan, a shiver going down my spine at the thought. "And I'd never know what I'd be missing out on. I mean, I've given myself orgasms before, but when someone else gives them to you, especially a man you are head over heels crazy about, it's a completely different experience."

River returns to the table, and I go silent on that matter. "Thanks for dinner."

"You're welcome," he replies, taking Bella's hand and kissing it. "It's been nice to have a few days of no drama."

"What do you think is going to happen with the Lost Lions MC?" I ask, frowning.

"They'll strike next. We made them look weak in that bar fight, so they're bound to retaliate. That's why it's important that the women and children are kept safe. You are the first thing they'll try to use against us."

"That's scary. If they did anything to Julian, I would kill them myself with my bare hands."

Bella's eyes widen. "Looks like you are a little like your brother after all."

"Nothing is going to happen to Julian, or to any of you," River promises us both. "We've got our security up, and eyes everywhere. Romeo is thinking they might strike Devil's Play—that's why we have Damon and the prospects there now. Blaze is driving around checking the perimeters of the business and the clubhouse."

I had no idea they were doing any of those things, but because I'm not a member I'm not really privy to those. Which sucks because if anyone should be a member, I should. Just because I don't have a penis between my legs, I'm not allowed to know. At least

I know now how important it is for Damon to be at the club, and he's not just there for the sake of it. He's making sure our MC is there in case Gio, Tatum, or any of their MC members show up to cause trouble.

River pauses, muttering a curse as he checks his phone. "Well, Romeo was right. They did show up at Devil's Play."

"What?" I whisper-yell. "Is Damon okay? Do we need to go there now?"

"He's fine, he handled it," he says, and the pride in his tone surprises me. "There was a bit of a fight, but the men were escorted off the premises."

Shit.

What if they'd gone to the club last night? If anything had happened to Bella and Julianna, it would have been my fault.

"I'm sorry we just showed up there," I say, wincing as I realize why they weren't happy with it. "I dragged them out, so it was on me, and I can see now how irresponsible it was."

"At least you didn't go alone," he replies, tightening his jaw. "And Damon was there. But yes, please call one of us before you plan on doing anything like that, just in case the Lost Lions MC is watching."

"I will," I promise. "And there's something I need to tell you."

"What?" he asks, sounding less than amused.

"I replied to Tatum. I thought that maybe I could get some intel that you guys could use—"

"You're trying to put me in a fucking grave this

month, aren't you?" River growls, shaking his head. "Why would you do that?"

"It's not like I told him anything," I argue, sliding him my phone. "But I did get him to confirm why he's here. He wants to find out who killed Robert, and he and his MC were kicked out of their last town by the cops."

River reads the texts, scowling. "Do not contact him again, do you hear me?" And then he suddenly smiles, which is even scarier than his angry face. "And you know what? You're Damon's problem now, so you can tell him about this little situation."

My jaw drops. "I'm Damon's *problem*? Not his blessing? Or gift? His problem?"

Bella hides her grin with her hand, and River simply shrugs, as if this realization has suddenly set him free.

"You could just admit that my information is useful," I say, scowling.

He tilts his head to the side. "Okay, yes, it is. But you are still reckless and—"

"And Damon's problem."

Asshole.

It's late when Damon picks me up, but I don't mind. I bring a bag with everything I need and plan to leave a few things at his, such as a toothbrush, shampoo and conditioner, bodywash, and a change of clothes. It's quiet when we get to the joint clubhouse, but I see Leif having a smoke outside.

"Hey," I greet him with a smile. "How are you?"

"Not too bad," he replies, eyes darting between Damon and me. "Just got in, so about to eat something and head to bed."

"Me, too," Damon replies, pulling me inside.

Wait, did Damon mean eat something?

Is he thinking the same thing I am?

I also wonder if Echo is into Vikings. Maybe we could set those two up.

"How was the club?" I ask Damon once we're inside his bedroom. "I heard the Lost Lions MC showed up."

"They did. I handled it," he replies, and I notice his cheek is a little red and swollen, but he otherwise looks unharmed.

"Was Tatum there?"

"Nope."

I put my bag in the corner of his room and take off my sandals. He stays silent and when I turn back around, he's watching me like a lion stalking its prey.

"You want something?" I ask, sitting down on the edge of the bed.

I need to tell him about Tatum, but I might wait until he's had his way with me. I know exactly what he wants, because I want it, too. I slowly lean back and spread my legs, showing off my panties as my linen dress rides up my thighs.

"Fucking hell," he whispers, a small smile playing on his lips. "How did I get so lucky?"

"You took a chance," I reply, pulling my dress

and bra off, and sitting there in my panties. He strips down and comes over to me, pushing me back and kissing me deeply.

I could get used to this life.

Several orgasms later, I'm lying on his chest and catching my breath. He kisses my fingers, my knuckles, and then the scars on my wrist.

I instantly freeze, feeling extremely vulnerable in this moment. Although I don't let my scars define me, they show how hurt and in pain I was at one stage in my life.

"You know I'm always here for you, no matter what, right?" he whispers, placing another kiss on the slightly raised skin. "No matter what."

"I know," I reply, swallowing hard.

But when he doesn't say anything further, I relax. He accepts me, and even my dark past.

And I hope he knows how much that means to me. I know I can be a lot, but he doesn't make me feel that way. And speaking of.

"By the way, I did something, and River got angry but then told me to tell you because apparently I'm your problem now."

He stills. "What the hell did you do?"

I tell him.

His fingers twitch on my skin, and he looks at me like he wants to kill me.

I run my hand over his dick, silently reminding him of the great sex we just had.

"Corey, don't fucking text him again," he demands in a low tone. "I'm serious."

I yawn. "I know, I won't. I found out what I could." And I proved that I can be useful, and not just some damsel in distress.

"If anything happened to you—"

"It won't," I promise.

Closing my eyes, I squeeze him tightly and fall asleep.

Feeling safe.

Julianna is in the kitchen the next morning, and hands me Julian. She's always moving between both clubhouses, and I don't know how she manages to stay organized, but she does.

"Did you sleep well?" she asks, trying to keep a straight face.

"I did, yes," I reply, lip twitching. "Where is everyone?"

"Romeo sent the prospects out to run some errands, and I'm getting someone to come in today and clean the place," she says, watching me hold her son. "You are so good with him."

"I adore him."

"And he, you," she replies, smiling down at him. "And considering you are here, I'm guessing things are going well with Damon."

"Yes." I smile. "But it's early days, so I don't want to jinx it."

She laughs softly. "I don't think you have to worry

about that. It's easy to see that you're both crazy about each other. We've all seen it ever since that party, when he kissed you and River attacked him for it."

"Yeah, I try not to remember the second part," I admit.

"I'll bet. But look how far you've come. You're spending the night with Damon, and he's alive. What a miracle."

"You know what, it really is a miracle," I agree, waving bye to Julian as I hand him back to her. "Is there anything you need me to do around here? I've got nothing going on today, so feel free to put me to work."

"If you can stay here while the cleaner comes, that would be great. We have a charity run on this weekend too, so if you want to help with the organization that would be ideal. We wanted to cancel with everything going on, but the proceeds are going to the children's hospital, and it's going to look bad on us if we suddenly pull out."

"Do you think the Lost Lions MC will show up?" I ask, frowning. "At a charity event?"

"We wouldn't put it past them, even if it's just them trying to intimidate us."

Damon steps into the kitchen, freshly showered and wearing a pair of light blue jeans and a white T-shirt. He runs his hand through his dark, still-wet hair, and I just want to drag him back into the bedroom, he looks that good. "Good morning, ladies."

"Good morning," Julianna says, pulling out her phone from her dress pocket as it starts to ring. "Excuse me, Romeo is calling me."

She steps outside and Damon comes over to pepper my face with kisses. "I have to go help Romeo with some things, so I can drop you back now."

"Julianna asked if I can stay while the cleaner is here."

He stills. "Alone?"

"I guess so."

He shakes his head. "No, I don't like that."

Julianna pokes her head in. "I didn't think you would. Romeo said you can stay here until the cleaner leaves, then lock the place up and head over to the Devils clubhouse after that. He wants you to go into the custom motorcycle shop with him. He's getting a new bike."

"Fuck yes." Damon grins, obviously more than happy to do that errand. "All right, sounds good."

She takes her leave, and Damon and I stare at each other. "What time is the cleaner coming?"

"In thirty minutes," I say, checking my watch. "Why?"

"So we're alone in the clubhouse for that time? There's a lot I can do in thirty minutes…"

He comes for me, and I playfully run away, laughing as he stalks me through the clubhouse until we end up in the living room. He spins me around so my back is to his front, and kisses the side of my neck, sending shivers down my whole body.

And then he bends me over the couch and lifts my dress up, pulling down my panties.

And he's right.

There is *a lot* he can do in thirty minutes.

Chapter Twenty-Three

Damon

We're at the custom motorcycle shop when we see them. We may know why they're here, but we don't know what they plan on doing. We do know that they've been patient and biding their time. They've rented out an Airbnb where they are staying for now, so at least it's short-term accommodation. Hopefully they get the hell out of our town soon enough.

They are getting off their bikes just as we are getting on ours, about to leave to head home.

"Well, what do we have here?" Gio comments, rubbing his hands together. They have a few more men than us, but I don't care. Romeo, River, and I are a good team and could take them.

"Hello there, brother. Nice to see you again."

"Tatum," River replies, tone dark as ever. "Why don't you just do what you came here to do so you can get the fuck out of here?"

Tatum laughs without humor. "Admit that you killed our father."

River gives nothing away, blue eyes unflinching. "Well, that's not going to happen. Robert didn't even want you—he raised me instead. So I don't know what you want. Daddy issues much?"

Tatum lunges for him, but Gio holds him back.

"I know you killed him!" Tatum yells, pointing at River.

"You don't know anything," River fires back. "We are not your family. We want nothing to do with you. And if you don't leave, you're going to end up with your father. Underground. At least then he will finally spend some time with you."

Fucking ouch.

Tatum has a full-blown tantrum at that, screaming and trying to go after River, and Gio and two other men try to hold him back, but he gets away and lunges for River with his fists, eyes wild.

River was anticipating it, though, and gives him a hook shot to one of his kidneys. Tatum drops, and we all stand there and watch him. My hands clench and I'm ready to jump in if needed.

"We're not leaving until the truth comes out," Tatum gasps, slowly pushing himself off the ground.

"Your funeral," Romeo states.

We get on our bikes and ride out.

I was waiting to see if Tatum said anything about Corey, but it doesn't seem like she is his priority, which is a good thing. He needs to leave her the hell alone and keep her out of all this. She's been through enough without having another asshole family member around. Her dad wasn't a good man, her mother doesn't talk to her, her brother died, and now her half brother needs to leave her in peace. His actions today prove he was only trying to use her.

River is the only one in that family who has ever truly cared for her, and I really respect him for that.

"What's our plan?" I ask Romeo when we get back to the clubhouse, still standing around our now-parked motorcycles.

Because we need one. Or this is just going to drag out, and they aren't going to leave. I have to wonder if Gio is really here just for Tatum, or if he has ulterior motives. My guess is the latter, and we need to find out what those are. They obviously have no place to go, but I don't care where they end up, as long as it's out of here.

"We can't keep sitting around," Romeo muses, sharing a look with River. "I think it's time we taught them a lesson. We aren't an MC they can fuck with, and they have no power here."

River flashes his teeth. "What did you have in mind?"

"I think we're going to need all hands on deck for this one," Romeo comments, gaze going back to River, and then to me. "I think we need to go all motherfucking out."

He's got my attention now.

"Call Jag in," he demands. "Ask him if he's found anything yet. And then tonight we'll call all the men in and agree on a plan. The women will need to be in lockdown and kept safe," he continues.

Fuck.

"When?" I ask.

"Tomorrow," he replies. "We can't give them time to one-up us."

I head inside to find Corey sitting outside in the sunshine reading a book. She looks so peaceful I consider not interrupting her, but then as if she could sense me, she looks over and smiles. "You're back!"

"I am," I reply, kissing the top of her head and sitting in the chair next to her. "We ran into the Lost Lions MC at the bike shop. I think shit is about to hit the fan."

She slides her sunglasses on top of her red hair. "What happened?"

I give her a quick rundown.

"Fucking Tatum," she mutters, closing her book with a loud clap. "He didn't even know Robert—so why can't he let this go?"

"We might be going into lockdown tomorrow," I tell her quietly, reaching over to take her hand. "I need you to be safe and listen to whatever Romeo decides."

Because if Tatum comes for anyone, I have a feeling it could be Corey. He'd feel entitled to her, even though he has nothing to do with her, and doesn't seem to give a shit.

End of the day, she's still his sister, and if he gets the opportunity to use her, I have no doubt that he will.

"Yes, of course. I'll do whatever I need to. Are you all going to be safe, though? I don't know what I'd do if something happened to you," she says, brow furrowing.

"I'll be fine," I promise. "As long as I know that you are somewhere safe."

"Is there anything I can do to help?" she asks, getting up and sitting on my lap, resting her head against my shoulder. "You can use me as bait, or whatever. If I can help, I will."

"I just told you I need you safe and you are offering yourself up as bait?"

She shrugs, a little sheepishly. "I just mean that I'm here for whatever you guys need. This is my family, too."

"I know." She's a ride-or-die chick, but I just need her to stay out of trouble while I handle this shit with the rest of the men.

"Are you going to leave us with a gun? We might need a gun," she says suddenly, and I can't help it, I laugh.

"Do you know how to use a gun?" I ask her.

She lifts her head and looks me in the eye. "River is my brother—what do you think?"

Right.

Of course.

I leave her to read her book and start getting ready for war.

Chapter Twenty-Four

Corey

"So we just have to hide out?" I ask, frowning at Julianna and Bella. "Surely there's something else we can do to help?"

I know Damon just wants me to sit here and look pretty tomorrow night, but I want to be useful. And I know they don't want me to message Tatum anymore, but what if I can get something else out of him?

"We just need to stay away so the other men can't use us as leverage," Bella explains, sighing. "River basically told me I'm his weakness, and he can't let them use his weakness against him."

I purse my lips. "Wow, my brother has a way with words. You aren't just his weakness—you're his strength, too."

"He did say that also," she admits, grinning.

"Well, we have the most important job, which is to make sure Julian is safe," Julianna adds, tucking her blonde hair back behind her ear. "I don't love hiding either, trust me, but Bella is right. We can't let them use us. And if we are safe the men will be able to do what they need to do with clear minds."

"The whole thing is crazy—do we even know what their plan is?" I ask, looking to Julianna, who is the most likely to know.

"We will decide tonight when we go to church," she says, glancing between us. "But I don't know if I can tell you every detail, especially if you aren't happy with staying behind."

I know that comment was aimed at me, and fair enough. "It's not that I have FOMO or anything. I just would help if given the opportunity."

"We know," she and Bella say at the same time.

"Who is staying with us, then?" I ask, knowing they aren't going to leave us without someone staying behind to protect us.

"I'm not sure, but it will have to be someone they trust."

Jeremiah, one of the Devils MC members, sticks his head into the lounge room where we are all congregating. "What are you three whispering about?"

"Come and sit down and find out," I tell him.

He grins and steps inside. He's wearing his staple leather pants, a black tank top, and one of those chain belts I haven't seen anyone else in this decade wear. "Okay, what's the gossip? Is this about Damon and Corey? Because we all know already. And yes, some of us are jealous."

I open my mouth, then almost choke on my words. "What?"

"Damon has a hot, younger old lady," he replies, shrugging. "And he got one that was off-limits. We love forbidden fruit."

I cover my mouth with my hand, both amused and horrified. "Please don't refer to me as forbidden fruit ever again. Or talk about me like I'm not sitting right here."

Although I get a secret thrill at being called Damon's old lady. I know I shouldn't, but I love it. Being known as his is something I've wanted for a long time. Not that I'd ever admit that out loud.

Jeremiah puts his hands up in surrender. "Sorry, it's a compliment."

Jag walks in eating a mango, speaking of fruit, which makes us all laugh. "What?" he asks.

Diamond walks in after him, and it's like our meeting's turned into a freaking party. I leave the room to go and find Damon, who is outside having a chat with Romeo. Not wanting to disturb them, I head into the kitchen and start making a platter for everyone to munch on.

We need this time with all of us together tonight.

"What have you got there?" Damon asks, hugging me from behind and pushing my hair off my neck so he can kiss me there. My fucking favorite.

"Just feeding the masses," I reply on a sweet sigh. "I came looking for you but didn't want to interrupt."

He picks up a grape and pops it into his mouth,

making a satisfying crunch. "Just working a few things out."

That's all he gives me.

But I'm not going to ask for any details until they've laid out their official plan tonight.

He helps me finish the platter and take it back out to the living room, where Jeremiah is showing off his dance moves to a song playing from his phone. We put the platter down on the coffee table and sit down to enjoy the show. He's not a bad dancer, to be honest, but then Diamond joins in and puts him to shame. I try not to look, but also don't want to *not* look, as he does a little grind movement that is pretty damn hot.

"Okay, I'm not as good as Diamond, but I'm not bad," Jeremiah then tells Julianna, who is picking up some fruit from the table with a grin on her face. "Don't underestimate me. Ooh, food."

"I didn't say you weren't a good dancer," she replies, laughing. "I just asked if you could dance, because I've never seen you dance."

"Well, now you know," he says, winking at her.

"You put more mango on the platter," Jag says, smiling up at me, his green eyes lit up. "You are seriously the best, you know that?"

I look over at Damon, who instead of being angry like he usually would be, is looking over at me with pride in his eyes. I suppose that's the difference with me openly being with him. Before, the men were a threat because they could take me. But now that I'm his, he can appreciate how well I get along with his MC brothers.

Love the man, love the club, right?

Except I already loved the club.

Damon being in it is just a bonus.

When my phone buzzes with a text, my eyes widen when I see it's from Tatum. This time, I show Damon right away.

Tatum: Come meet me?

"Surely we can use this to help us."

He hands my back my phone. "Maybe. Don't reply for now, and we will come up with a plan."

I nod, happy that he's listening and considering my offer. I might not be able to be on the front lines, but I can still help, and that's all I wanted to do.

We all sit around talking shit for some time, until Romeo and River call all the men to church. Julianna joins them. Bella and I sit back with Julian and wait to see what is decided.

I already feel like I know how this is going to go. The men are going to ambush them, maybe kidnap Tatum, or maybe even kill him.

I know I should feel sadness at this, but Tatum is a stranger to me. He's not my family.

And now he's threatening the people that are.

I won't stand for it.

And if the time comes, I'll do whatever I can to protect what's mine.

Chapter Twenty-Five

Damon

The next evening comes around and it's go time. We have decided to put the women and Julian at the new clubhouse, because it's less known and frequented. We also have high fences and are on a hill, which is a good advantage point. If there is an emergency, we also have a bulletproof basement they could hide in, and one that isn't easy to locate. Romeo wants to leave two men with them, so we decided on Leif and Jag. They are going to be on call for anything we may need and will also be on security watch.

And the best part of this plan? We don't have an exact plan. We are going to go find them and take advantage of whatever opportunistic situation presents itself. Ideally, we'd like to be able to take Tatum or Gio hostage and give them a little time with River in our dungeon. We can't have them in our town, making everyone feel unsafe.

"Oh shit," Jag murmurs, looking up away from his phone. "I think I found something."

"What?" Romeo asks, brow furrowing.

"I've been going through social media and public records, trying to find what Tatum's been up to since he turned eighteen, and he has a kid. He's been hiding him—the kid doesn't have his name."

Romeo and River share a look.

"I'm not saying we should hurt a five-year-old child," Jag clarifies, clearing his throat. "But we could use that as leverage. As to whether he even cares about his kid, that's another story."

"I wouldn't harm an innocent kid," Romeo says, and we all nod in agreement. "But if we need to use that, we'll have to."

"At the end of the day that is Corey's nephew," I point out. "Speaking of Corey, she wants to help by trying to get information we can use from Tatum."

Romeo turns his head to me. "And how do you feel about that?"

"I think she wants to be useful, and I think she can be," I reply, backing my woman.

River nods. "I agree, as long as you keep her safe."

The threat is in his tone. He's giving me freedom to make choices regarding her, but if harm comes to her, he's going to kill me.

They leave it to me to handle. As long as she remains in the clubhouse, safe, I have no problem with her helping in that way. I didn't miss the way her face lit up when I said we'd consider it.

"You look all sexy in black," Corey comments a little while later, as she steps into my bedroom as I'm getting all my weapons ready. She eyes my usually hidden collection of guns and knives in my wardrobe. "Okay, I had no idea that was in there."

"That's the point." I grin, bending down to slide a knife into a strap around my shin. When I look over at her, she's staring at me with that glimmer in her eye that I've been getting to know too well. "What?"

She reaches up to push my hair off my forehead. "I don't know, you in your shady getup and weapons is really doing it for me."

I laugh and cup her face. "I love you."

I've been wanting to tell her, and this is the moment. I want her to know how much she means to me. If I know anything, it's how short life can be and I need to tell her how I feel.

Her eyes widen in surprise, and her throat works as she swallows. "I love you, too. But you already know that because I accidentally said it before."

She's so damn cute.

"I don't know what's going to happen tonight, so I just wanted to tell you that," I say, lowering my head for a kiss. "But I'm sure it's going to be fine."

I say "fine" like Ross from *Friends*.

I hope she doesn't notice.

"Okay, why don't you message Tatum now and keep him talking? Stay by your phone. I'll text you with what you should ask him, and we will see how forthcoming he is with information."

I should probably run this new plan by Romeo and River, but like River told me, she's my responsibility now, and I know how important it is to her to feel useful. I decide we can just see how this plays out for now.

She nods. "Okay, I won't let you down."

"You could never," I reply, my tone raspy. "I hope you know how incredible you are, Corey. You are strong, you are an asset. And I'm so fucking proud to have you standing with me."

Her eyes shine with tears, and she takes a deep breath. I think she needed to hear that, and I will remind her every fucking day if I have to.

We share a long hug and some more kisses before we leave the bedroom.

The men meet out front, all fully loaded and ready to go. I must admit, we do look pretty badass.

"Look after them," I tell Jag and Leif, looking between them.

They both nod. "You know I will," Jag replies, slapping me on the shoulder. "We got this."

"I will guard them with my life," Leif promises.

And then we get on our bikes and ride off. I don't know how this is going to go, but I do know that we aren't leaving until we get what we want from them.

Which is for them to get the fuck out of here.

Jeremiah and Diamond go alone to do a stakeout and watch the Lost Lions MC to see what else they can find, while the rest of us get ready for war. After about an hour, Tatum leaves the rest of his MC and rides off somewhere alone, so we send Blaze after him in a car to follow him. Having Tatum separated from his MC puts us at an advantage.

Corey: Damon, I think Tatum is going to go to my mom's house. He texted that he needed to talk to her!

Shit.

Damon: I will handle it.

The rest of us are close by, hiding out in an empty warehouse that we own, our bikes out of sight.

"Corey thinks that Tatum is going to go to her mom's house," I tell Romeo, who mutters a curse.

"Blaze is on him. And Jeremiah says there are about fifteen men still in the house," Romeo says, looking at his phone screen. "Tatum has left, and the rest of them are just hanging around, it looks like. They're drinking and talking shit. Only problem is, they've brought a few women from town over to party with." He pauses, and then mutters a curse. "Okay, bigger problem. One of those women is Rosalind."

"Shit," River replies, scowling. "I wish I could say I'm surprised she's partying with the enemy, but no, I'm not."

I can literally see the regret and disgust flash in

Romeo's eyes. "Okay, no women get hurt. Someone will need to get them out safely."

"Even the wicked witch?" River asks, jaw tightening.

"Yes, especially the wicked witch," Romeo replies in a dry tone, pushing off the wall and walking to the entrance of the warehouse. We're all a little on edge, and I'm sure just like me, he wants this over with so we can go back to our women and on with our usual lives.

He turns around just as his phone vibrates and he quickly answers it. "Yeah? What? Yes, stop him! We are on the way."

"What?" I ask, standing to alert.

"Blaze said Tatum is heading out of town," he says, straddling his motorcycle. He turns to River. "I think Corey's right—he's going to your mother's house."

Fuck!

Of course.

Tatum's dad was married to River's mother, so why wouldn't he try to use that? He wouldn't give a shit about Lisa, so I wouldn't put it past him to hurt her in revenge for what happened to Robert.

"Blaze is going to try to stop him, or at the least follow him there," he says, pausing. "Fuck, what do you want to do, River?"

River stays calm as always, but underneath I know that he is fucking furious. "I'll go alone. We can't go now and leave the clubhouse with just two men and the rest of us out of town. You guys go ahead with the original plan. I'll go to my mom's."

And with that, he rides off.

Romeo starts to pace, and I know he's not a fan of how the night is starting out. "I don't like us all being spread out like this."

"I mean, if we get Tatum, do we need to storm their place?" I ask, and the two of us share a long glance.

"Fuck it, everything has changed. Let's go and get Tatum. I'll send Jeremiah back to the clubhouse in case we need him there."

I nod, agreeing with our president's decision.

If we get Tatum, we have some leverage.

And with him being alone right now, it's our best and easiest bet. Not that the giant lug won't go down without a fight.

But the women will be safe, and we don't have to worry about any of them getting harmed in the crossfire.

Tatum wanted a fight, and now we're going to give him one.

Chapter Twenty-Six

Corey

Tatum: I need to speak to your mom. If you'd met up with me, we could have gone together.

Corey: What? Are you going there now?

Is that what he means?

Shit, shit, shit.

I text Damon, but Tatum doesn't reply further. I was right, and I hope that it will help my mom stay safe. For all our baggage, I'd hate myself if I let something bad happen to her.

And then Jeremiah showing up alone scares the shit out of me. I have a million questions for him.

"Why are you here? Are they safe? What happened?" I ask, wrapping my arms around him. "Tell me everything."

He smirks and looks around, gently removing my

hands. "I'll tell you when Julianna is here. Where is she?"

"Changing Julian. Julianna!"

She comes down with Julian in her arms. "What's going on?"

Jeremiah looks at me, and I can tell he's about to say something that I'm not going to like. "You were right, Corey. Tatum was heading out of town, alone, in the direction of where your mom lives. We think he's heading there. So the plan has changed—we're going after Tatum and not bothering with the Lost Lions MC for now."

"He told me he is going there," I confirm.

"Shit. Okay, but everyone else is fine. Another thing, Julianna. Rosalind was there partying with the Lost Lions MC."

Julianna scowls, shaking her head. "Probably trying to get her own president. Will she be safe there?"

"Yeah, don't worry," he assures her.

Jeremiah updates everyone else. Julianna calls up her family to let them know what's going on. The older members of the MC have stepped back since Julianna and Romeo took over, leaving the new generation to run things and embrace the change of joining the two MCs, but that doesn't mean that they might not be targeted.

"So do we have eyes on their place?" Jag asks, frowning.

Jeremiah grins. "Yeah, we do. I set up that camera you gave me in the bushes. So we can see who is coming in and out."

Jag smiles and offers him a fist bump. "Love your work. Let me go and set it up so we can watch it on the screen. Everyone stay indoors. Don't go outside."

We all decide we're hungry so we head to the kitchen. I wonder if River called Mom and told her that Tatum is coming to her house. He might not have bad intentions, but knowing him that is a very naive thought. I decide to send her a text. I know we haven't spoken in a long time, but now seems like the time to reach out. It's for her safety.

Corey: Hey, Mom. Did River call you?

I then realize she probably doesn't even have my new number, which is sad in itself.

Corey: It's Corey, by the way.

You know, your only daughter.

Mom: Yes, he called me. He's on his way here. I'm fine. I don't think Tatum would hurt me.

She didn't think Robert would hurt her, either.

I stare at my phone, but she doesn't say anything else. And you know what? It does hurt. I push it away and pretend that I don't need her or want her love and affection, but deep down of course I do. Who wouldn't? I guess I just don't see how she doesn't care about me or want to know how I'm doing. Maybe that's why I don't want to have any kids of my own.

"Corey, do you want some?" Bella asks, breaking me out of my miserable thoughts.

I turn to see her holding a plate of sandwiches out for me. "Yes, please."

Leif sits down at the table with us, taking up a lot of space. His hair is in braids, like a true Viking, and I wonder who did them for him.

"Sad you're missing out on the action?" I ask, making conversation.

He shrugs his broad shoulders. "I'm just happy to help out however they need me to."

"Good attitude to have," I reply. My eyes go to his phone when a message pops up on the screen, and because I'm nosy I look at what it says.

And then I pretend that I didn't see it at all.

"So, how long do you think until they get back? Tomorrow?" I ask the table, while Leif grabs his phone and tucks it away in his pocket.

"Probably," Jag replies, standing up. "I'm going to go check the cameras. Jeremiah, do a perimeter check, will you?"

"Sure thing," Jeremiah says, leaving.

And then it's just Julianna, Bella, me.

And a traitor.

I know I need to play my next moves very carefully and make it seem like I didn't just read what I did.

So I stay calm, and try to keep my energy the same. People can sense energy, and if mine turns cold or scared, he will know that something is up, and that I was quick enough to read his text.

"Does anyone want a drink?" I ask, while I quickly send Damon a text.

"Sure," Leif replies, while Julianna and Bella politely decline.

"Beer?" I offer, but he shakes his head. Of course he doesn't want a beer—he needs his wits about him with all the betrayal he's about to commit. "Soda?"

"Yes, please."

I grab two cans and set one down in front of him, the other for me.

"If I sit here like this, I'm going to go crazy," Julianna announces, standing up and leaving the table.

"I'll go check on her," Bella says, following.

And I'm left with Leif.

That motherfucker.

And Damon still hasn't replied.

I tap my black-tipped nails on the table, and then sit back and open my drink, which makes a fizzing noise. Leif does the same, taking a sip and then stretching his large neck from side to side.

My phone buzzes and I rush to check it, thinking it might be Damon.

Or my mom.

But it's neither of them.

Echo: Hey, just checking in. Romeo had us close Devil's Play and told me to stay home, so I guess something is going on.

I type furiously.

Corey: Yeah, it's a giant shit show. Stay home and lock your doors. Trust no one.

No one is safe.

I doubt they'd go after Echo, who they would see as just an employee of the club, but you never know. Anyone I care about right now needs to just be safe.

Echo: Oh dear. Yes, I'm home catching up on *The Last Kingdom*. Call me if you need anything.

Corey: Right back at you.

"*The Last Kingdom*, now that is a good show," I say to myself.

Leif nods slightly in agreement. He's so calm and collected.

It annoys me.

He played me, all of us, just like Rosalind did, and it makes me angry. An image of her pops into my head, and for once it doesn't fill me with instant panic and anxiety. My therapy sessions must be paying off.

Jeremiah returns and checks on everyone. When he sees all is good, he goes to observe the security cameras with Jag, once again leaving Leif and me alone.

I can't let him get away with this. I'm the only one that knows the truth, so it's up to me to make it right. He's not going to get away with betraying all the people I love. I grit my teeth, the anger of the situation hitting me.

How dare he do this to us?

"I'm going to go and get changed into something warmer," I lie.

Instead, I go into Damon's room, open his secret gun stash, and take a handgun. And some bullets.

And then I brace myself to go back into that kitchen and face him.

The text that popped up on his phone was from an unsaved number, but it said:

We are ready and waiting for them. Just waiting on your signal. They won't know what hit them.

Well, now he's not going to know what hit *him*.

I tuck the gun in the waistband of my jeans and walk back out to the kitchen. Leif is still alone and on his phone.

I turn off the safety of the gun and come up behind him.

"You're with the Lost Lions MC, aren't you?" I say, and he turns around, eyes flaring when he sees the pistol pointed at him. "I saw the text message. You are giving them inside information. Don't try to lie about it!"

"Corey—"

"I'm not going to let you get anyone I love hurt!" I seethe. "And if that means me killing someone, then so be it."

He stands up, with his hands in the air, facing me. His eyes are wide and filled with surprise. "Let me explain—"

The time for explaining is long gone.

I lower the gun and shoot him in the foot.

That will slow him down until I can decide what I want to do with him.

"Fuck!" he yells, dropping to the floor, just as Jag walks into the room, his expression turning to one of shock.

Tilting my head to the side, I point the gun at Leif's other foot. Then he definitely won't be going anywhere, will he?

"Corey? What the hell are you doing?" Jag growls, taking the gun from my hands. "You shot him? What is going on here?"

"Yes, I did, and I'll do it again! He's a traitor, he's with the other MC, and he's giving them information! He's probably going to try to kill us all!"

Jag pauses, looks at Leif.

And then he tips his head back and laughs.

"What's so fucking funny?" I snap, just as Julianna rushes in. She's alone, so Bella probably has Julian upstairs.

"Oh my god, Leif, are you okay? What happened?" she asks, rushing over to him. She takes her hoodie off and uses it to try to stop the bleeding.

"Let him bleed out! He's a traitor," I tell her.

"Corey shot him," Jag says, and I'm about to slap the amusement on his face.

Julianna pauses and turns to me. "Why do you say that?"

I tell them about the texts I read.

Leif looks like he's about to pass out, staring at the blood all over the floor and kitchen cabinets. Does he not like blood? Not a surprise since he's a coward.

Jag pulls me against him, holding me as I attempt to lunge for Leif. "Corey, let us explain. Leif isn't a traitor. Well, he is. Just not to us. He's on our side, but the Lost Lions MC thinks he's on theirs."

"They tried to recruit him," Julianna explains, turning to look at me. "So we got him to go with it and act as a kind of undercover agent. I'm sorry, Corey, we didn't tell anyone else. We didn't think anything like this would happen."

Oh.

Shit.

Chapter Twenty-Seven

Damon

We ride in formation, speeding down the highway.

It's not long until we come across Blaze's car, parked on the side of the road, right near Corey's mother's house. There's a motorcycle there, too.

Shit.

We all come to a stop, and only then do we see the two men rolling in the grass, beating the shit out of each other. I wonder if Blaze ran him off the road—regardless, he did what he said he would.

He stopped him.

River gets off his bike first and runs to him, grabbing Tatum and taking Blaze's place. The rest of us stand by.

River hits him in the jaw, then kicks him in the stomach. Tatum still stands, trying to punch River back, fists swinging. River is faster, though, and ducks before getting him in the nose, and then knocks him out in two more blows. I approach and hand him some zip ties from my bike, and he ties Tatum up, and drags him into the car.

It was a close call, but we got him. Now to get home and make sure everyone is safe there.

We follow the car all the way back, just to make sure Tatum doesn't wake up and try anything. When we pull into the clubhouse, the rumble of our bikes loud as ever brings Jag out the front. I pull my helmet off and face him. He gives me a thumbs-up. All is good.

Fucking wonderful.

I worried that Gio would storm our clubhouse instead, with only a few of our members there. But it looks like Leif did his job and kept him at bay by letting him think we were still going through with showing up at their place. And with Corey's information, we were able to get to Tatum in time. We all owe her.

Everything somehow worked out and I, for one, am glad.

I just need Corey in my arms, and life will be good again.

For now, anyway.

River and Romeo carry Tatum into the garage, and the rest of us head inside.

"There's one little thing," Jag says to me as we walk through the front door.

"What is it?" I ask, stopping when I come across Leif sitting in the lounge room, his foot resting on the arm of the leather couch. There's a blood-soaked bandage around it.

"What the hell happened to you?" I ask, frowning.

"Your old lady shot me," Leif says casually, opening a bar of chocolate and eating it, like it's just another fucking day.

"Corey?"

"Yes," comes her voice from behind me.

I turn and open my arms to her, and she runs into them. "You shot him?" I ask her, eyebrows rising.

She's okay.

I'm okay.

I don't care who she fucking shot.

"Yeah, long story," she says, dangling her arms around my neck and kissing my cheek. "I sent you a text about it, but you didn't reply, so I had to take matters into my own hands. I'm glad you are home."

"Me, too. Sorry, I have no idea where my phone went."

Romeo steps into the room beside me. "Fucking hell, Corey. Julianna told me what happened."

"He's alive, though," Corey says, pointing at him, like it makes it all okay. "At least I didn't shoot him in the head."

Romeo scrubs his hand down his face. "You are your brother's sister, you know that?"

"He's your brother, too," she reminds him. He sighs.

"I'll take Leif to see Dr. Shine," Jag offers, looking to Romeo for confirmation.

Romeo nods. "Yeah, take Jeremiah with you, though."

Jag rubs his hands together excitedly.

"Why do you look so happy?" Corey asks him.

"Have you seen Dr. Shine? She's hot," he replies, grinning. "Smoking hot."

"Dr. Shine is our connection at the hospital. She helps us out and doesn't ask any questions," Romeo explains.

"I remember hearing her mentioned before," Corey replies, looking over at Leif's foot. "But I pictured an old man, not a hot woman."

Jag helps Leif get up and supports him while he hops out of here. I turn to Corey and ask her to explain herself.

"Shit," I whisper after she's given me the rundown. "Of course you'd figure that all out."

She smiles, wincing. "I'm so sorry. I shouldn't have taken your gun and shot him, but I thought I was protecting the club. That has to count for something right? I didn't want to mess around in case he was going to hurt us. And Julian was in the house!"

It's hard to argue with that logic. I'm also in awe of her. How she handled the situation, how she protected everyone. She's strong, fierce, and a weapon in her own right. And I'd be lying if I said my cock wasn't hard right now. She clearly has a violent side—when it's justified.

"No more guns for you," is all Romeo says to that. But then he pauses on his way past her and touches her shoulder. "But thank you. You are one badass chick, you know that?"

Corey grins, and I shake my head, then grab her and kiss her.

"What's going to happen with Tatum?" she asks when she looks out the window toward the garage.

"We are going to get information out of him and use him for leverage. But we're going to move him out of here later tonight," I explain. "Our goal is to get something to use to make them all leave for good. And then we can be done with these assholes."

"Corey! I know you betrayed me!" Tatum calls out at the top of his lungs. He's outside, being taken into the garage. "I wouldn't have hurt her!"

Yeah, sure.

I take her away from the window. I know this must be hard for her.

We don't want him here because it's the first place they will come look for him.

And they *will* come.

So we need to be ready.

"How weird, my brother is in the garage, being tortured by my other brother," she muses, sighing.

It hits me then how hard this must be for her. She might not know, or be close to Tatum, but he is still her blood. "Are you okay?" I ask, brow furrowing.

Her chest rises sharply as she takes a breath. "Yeah, I'll be okay. The whole thing is pretty messed up. And I sent my mom a message when I found out that he was headed there."

"What did she say?" I ask her, rubbing her nape gently.

"She said she's fine, and she didn't think he would do anything to her. And that's it. No 'how are you,' no 'it's nice to hear from you.' No anything," she says, her hazel eyes sad.

"I'm sorry, Corey. Maybe she will sit on it for a while and reach out when she's in the right head space," I suggest, holding her against me. "And if not, it's her loss. She should be proud to have a daughter like you."

I don't know how she accepts her psychotic son but rejects Corey, who is sweet and loyal and talented and smart.

I will never understand it.

And it's so shitty that I have to try to protect her feelings from her own mother. The woman who birthed her, named her, and raised her.

"Thanks," she replies, looking up at me through her thick lashes.

Even sad, she is the most beautiful woman I've ever seen.

"You've got me now, and I'm always going to be here for you," I say, lifting her up in a bear hug and carrying her into our bedroom.

I know that nothing will stop the hurt from her relationship with her mother, but I can at least try to love her enough to make up for it. And maybe one day, they will be able to reconnect.

But until then, I got her.

With the adrenaline from today still pumping through my veins, I throw her on the bed, and lock the door behind me.

I'm going to show her just how much I missed her.

Chapter Twenty-Eight

Corey

The perks of the MC owning so many properties and businesses is that when you need to hide someone, you have the facilities to do so.

But before Tatum is long gone to an undisclosed location, with River as his number-one captor, I ask if I can have five minutes with him.

That doesn't go down well, but just like in most situations, I win.

"I'm going in with you," Damon states, as we stand by the garage door.

"Just stand here," I tell him, lifting my head to kiss him.

When I step inside, Tatum is sitting on the ground, bound and beaten. I have to admit, I do feel bad for him. At the end of the day, he is blood related to me, even if I don't know him.

"I thought I could trust you," he says without looking up. "But you're just like River, aren't you?"

"And you're just like our father," I return, with no heat in my tone. "You think you're avenging this great man. Robert was an abusive asshole, and while I don't know what happened to him, I'm glad he's dead."

"I just wanted to prove that River killed him. Don't you want that? He's your dad, too."

I sigh heavily. "What does it matter? He's gone now. But we're alive and we need to move on and live our lives. And to be honest, he wasn't a nice person, Tatum. He didn't even visit you, or support you, and the kids he did stay around for...well, we thought you got the better deal."

"He was still our father."

"Sometimes family is defined by loyalty, not blood. You're in an MC, you should know that."

"You're a traitor, and things aren't over yet, Corey. I'm not going to let this go."

And that's why I probably won't see him again.

"Tell Dad I said hi," is all I say before I walk back outside.

I know people say I'm a little like River, but the truth is, I'm not. Yes, I'll do what I need to protect the people I love, but from what I've heard the other men say, River seems to enjoy it. That, or he feels nothing at all. Maybe he can disassociate. Who knows?

But I can't relate to that. River's anger runs cold, where mine runs hot. My rage and violence are fueled by passion, and the desperate need to protect those that I love. I couldn't hurt just anyone.

Damon walks me back into the kitchen and wraps me in his arms. Did he think what I said was cold?

But then he tells me how much he loves me, and how strong I am.

And I know that I'm where I'm meant to be.

"I can't believe you shot Leif," Bella says, looking both horrified and on the verge of breaking out into laughter. "You are just full of surprises."

"Don't you dare tell me I'm like River, or I'm going to scream," I state, pushing my sunglasses up on my nose. We're both sitting outside enjoying our morning coffee together, and debriefing everything that happened yesterday.

She lets the laughter loose. "Is that what everyone is saying? Probably why I get along with both of you so well."

"I'm going to kill you."

"You going to shoot me, too?" she asks, trying to keep a straight face. I roll my eyes. "At least he's going to be fine. He's going to be walking in no time. At least that's what the hot doctor told him."

"Jag came back happier than I've ever seen him," Bella comments, taking a sip from her mug. "Happier than when he's eating a mango." She lowers her tone. "Have you seen how he eats one? You just know he's good at...certain things."

My eyes widen, because no lie, I had a similar

thought when I first watched him consume one. And *consume* is the right word. "Oh, definitely," I reply, wiggling my eyebrows. "You just know he's one of those men who enjoy it. He would devour you."

Not one drop would be left.

"Well, the good doctor might be in luck, then."

We both start laughing.

"What are you two whispering about?" Damon asks as he opens the sliding door and steps outside.

Damn, that was close.

"Nothing," I lie. "Just enjoying the sunshine. We can't go anywhere until these Lost Lions MC shenanigans are done with, so we are making the best of it. By the way, I can't wait for the pool at the new clubhouse. With the big garden, it will be beautiful, and I can't wait to use it."

"The new clubhouse has everything," Bella adds, scrolling on her phone. "It even has a playroom. A home theater. A spa. We will never have to leave that house."

"A playroom for just Julian until everyone else starts having kids," Damon says, looking over at Bella. "Are you guys next?"

Bella shrugs and plays coy. "Who knows? Maybe in a year or two. I'm not ready just yet."

"I'd like a few kids in a couple of years," Damon says, winking at me.

And it suddenly hits me that we've never had the conversation.

The one where I tell him I don't want any children.

At least I think I don't.

I envision a baby with his gray eyes and dark hair, and yeah, my heart melts a little, but not enough to commit. Of course he'd want children. He didn't have a good childhood, and I know he'd break generational curses to make sure that the cycle didn't repeat. He'd be a great father. I see him with Julian.

"What's wrong?" he asks, stroking my arm. "Corey?"

"I don't know if I want kids," I blurt out, turning to face him. "And it just hit me that we've never spoken about it. We probably should have."

"You don't want kids? Ever?" he asks, sounding surprised. "But you love kids. You are amazing with Julian."

"It's not that I don't like kids—I do. I love kids. I just never pictured myself having any. I thought I'd always just be the fun aunt, I don't know," I admit, wringing my hands together nervously.

He takes one of my hands and holds it in his. For safekeeping. "You have nothing but time to decide these things."

"But what if I don't change my mind?" I ask, because I feel like that's where he's going with this. He thinks I'll have a change of heart, and that maybe this is just a phase. But I've felt like this for a long time.

"We'll worry about it when we get there," he replies gently, playing it off.

But this is a big problem, and it could be a deal breaker for one of us. I don't know if it's something we should just hope works itself out. I don't want to fall more and more and get attached and then he says he wants a baby.

Would I have one just to keep him?

Sighing, I figure this is a conversation we need to have when we are alone, and once I have processed my thoughts on it.

"Okay," I reply, stroking his knuckles with my thumb. "But I think it's something we both need to get on the same page about."

How does one compromise in a situation like this?

I don't think you can. You either want the same thing, or you don't.

When I turn to ask Bella a question, I realize that she has quietly left and gone back inside. I don't blame her—I wouldn't want to be around a couple having this conversation, either.

"I agree," he replies, bringing my hand to his lips and placing a kiss there. "And we will. But it's not something we have to commit to right now, we have the time to figure it out. Together."

He's so sweet.

Maybe I could just have one child…

No, I wouldn't do that for anyone. I'd have to be a hundred percent sure, or it's just not fair to everyone else.

I feel unsettled after this conversation, because this isn't just something small.

This is huge.

This is a deal breaker for most, if not now, then perhaps somewhere down the line.

I have a lot to think about, but all I do know is that I don't want any other man.

I want him, and I have for the longest time. This is the man I couldn't escape, the one who, for whatever reason, kept calling out to me. No matter what was going on in my life, or how angry or annoyed I was at Damon, underneath it all, it was always him.

And now, I don't know what to do.

Chapter Twenty-Nine

Damon

Corey goes quiet after our conversation, and I have to admit that what she said caught me off guard. I watch her with Julian all the time, the way she lights up when she sees him, and dotes on him, and is forever rushing to steal him away from Julianna or Romeo. But I guess that doesn't mean she would definitely want her own, so this is a conversation I'm glad came up. I think she'd be a wonderful mother, but at the end of the day it's her choice.

I've always wanted children, ever since I can remember, but I also don't want to lose Corey. I guess I could always play the uncle role to all the MC members' kids. That wouldn't be so bad.

But I think it's fine to say that now. Years down the line, will I regret it?

Fucking hell.

I thought the hardest part of us getting together

was over and that it would be smooth sailing from now on, but of course that was naive of me. All relationships require work, compromise, and effort. And even though we are crazy about each other, ours will be no different.

I decide to let it go for now, we're knee-deep with Tatum, and I know that it's not going to be long until Gio figures out he's missing and makes his next move.

"Do you want to go out for breakfast or something? Before shit hits the fan," I suggest, and she lights up.

"Yes, I'd love that. Let me go and get ready."

I grab my phone—one of the men found it in the clubhouse parking lot—and I let Romeo know we're heading out for an hour and ask if we need to get anything on the way.

"I think we're good, just be diligent," he says, squeezing the bridge of his nose. "They still haven't found the camera Jeremiah planted, so we have eyes on them for now. They're all still there."

"Good." I nod, resting my hand on his shoulder. "It's all going to be fine."

He cracks a small smile. "Having a kid makes all this shit way more stressful. Normally I'd be in my element right now; instead I'm worried something might happen to Julian or Julianna. Or Corey or Bella."

"We won't let anything happen," I assure him.

And for a moment I wonder if maybe Corey is

right, and bringing a child into this environment isn't the best thing.

She comes out in a denim skirt and a tight white top, and suddenly I'm hungry for something else. Her wide smile as she holds on to her bag, ready to go, makes me unexplainably happy.

"Come on, let's get you fed, then," I say, wrapping my arm around her. "What are you in the mood for? There's that new place that does those fancy bagels and cake; I've been wanting to go there."

"Me, too, that sounds perfect."

We step outside just as a familiar car pulls up to park. And then a familiar blonde gets out of the car, her face turning sour when she sees me and Corey.

Fucking hell.

"What is she doing here?" I mutter, holding on to Corey tighter.

"So, now we know why you broke up with me," Melinda sneers, looking at Corey like she'd like to strangle her. "What, am I too old for you?"

I grit my teeth, trying to stay calm. "What do you want, Melinda? You aren't welcome here, and now is really not a good time."

"There will be no good time to tell you what I'm here to say," she says with an evil grin. A shiver goes down my spine at her smug expression.

"What?" I demand.

She puts her hand on her stomach. "I'm pregnant. And it's yours."

I feel Corey stiffen next to me, and I hold on to

her even tighter, panic taking over me. Is she serious? My blood turns to ice.

"I think you're full of shit. We used protection every time," I remind her. I'm not stupid, and I'm not out there having any kind of unprotected sex. Especially not with someone I wasn't even in a proper relationship with. And we only had sex a few weeks ago, how could she know already?

"Condoms aren't a sure thing," she replies in a dry tone. "And I told you I was on the pill, I know, but I'm pretty bad at remembering to take them."

This is the last thing I need right now, especially after the conversation I literally just had with Corey. Although I only slept with her a couple of times, Melinda is right in saying condoms don't always work, but I still think she's lying. It's all a little too convenient, and I don't trust her. But there's always that one percent chance that she's not. And that's what has me fucked up right now.

"Well, I guess you got what you want," Corey says from beside me, looking up with hurt hazel eyes I never want to see looking at me like this again. "Congratulations."

And then she turns around and walks back into the clubhouse.

Fuck.

I turn to Melinda. "I don't believe you, and until there's proof, it's going to stay that way."

"What proof could I possibly give you?" she asks,

a little too happy after witnessing Corey walking away from me.

"Proof that you actually are pregnant, and if you are, then a DNA test the second the baby is born."

What a fucking disaster this is. I'm usually so careful and keep everything so private, but I obviously made a huge mistake by ever having anything to do with Melinda.

And if she really is pregnant with my child, I'm going to be heartbroken, because this isn't the kind of mother I would have wanted for my firstborn. I can't believe how awful she is being, and how only now she's showing her true colors.

She holds out her hand. "I'm going to need some money, too. Appointments aren't cheap."

Of course she does.

"I tell you what, make an appointment and I'll come with you, and then I can see if you actually are pregnant," I suggest, not going to let her try to fool me.

She didn't even come with an ultrasound picture, nothing, and expects me to believe her? Especially after how she acted the last time I saw her, which now feels like a lifetime ago.

"Fine," she snaps, pulling her hand away. "I'll let you know."

And then she drives off, knowing exactly how much damage she has caused in my relationship in the last five minutes, and most likely loving every second of it.

Romeo comes out and stands next to me. "Corey is crying in there—what happened?"

"I've fucked up."

Even if she's not pregnant, and it's all a ruse, I've still fucked up.

I never should have touched that woman.

Chapter Thirty

Corey

"I should just let them be together and be happy. Damon can be a dad, like he always wanted, and I'll just be alone," I cry on Bella's shoulder.

"You know, she could be lying," Julianna says, as she rubs my back. "It's very early for her to be showing, and who's to say it's his? She's obviously obsessed with him, but he doesn't want her and she knows it. If she is pregnant, then we will have to deal with it for the child's sake, and be there for him or her, but I'd like to know if it really is his first."

"We won't know that for months, so what do I do in the meantime? Just pretend like everything is okay?" I ask, my lower lip trembling. "We just had a conversation about how I don't want kids but he does, and then this happens. I just want to go back to yesterday. It was a much simpler day."

Even after shooting Leif, I was still happier.

In just a few moments, everything has changed so much, and I truly feel heartbroken over the fact that she really could be carrying his child. But Julianna is right, she could also be making it up and trying to pin it on Damon.

I don't know what to believe, but until we get the proof, there's still a chance that it could be his.

And that's not going to be easy to let go.

A soft knock at the door has me wiping my tears. "Corey? Can I come in please?"

My first instinct is to tell him to go away, and that I don't want to see him. But I need to face this, and be brave, because this problem is not going anywhere.

"Do you want to talk to him now, or do you need more time?" Bella kindly asks me.

"I'll talk to him," I say, and Julianna opens the door.

He steps inside my bedroom looking like he's aged several years since this morning. The girls leave and close the door behind him.

"I'm so sorry, Corey," he starts off with, sitting down on my bed and looking over at me. "About everything. I don't know if it's true, but I'm going to find out. I might sound like an asshole, but if I'm being honest, I think she's making it up to get back at me for breaking up with her."

I don't know what to say. I feel numb, and like my body isn't my own. I look down at my wrists, remembering the last time I felt this way.

"She might be lying," I agree, wrapping my arms

around myself. "But if she's not, would you be happy? I mean, you said you wanted kids and this way you'd get one—"

"I wanted kids with you, Corey," he corrects, sliding closer to me and holding me. "I don't want kids with anyone else. And if you don't want them, that's okay. I'd rather not have them at all, then."

"But now you might," I point out, tears dripping down my cheeks. "I'm sorry, I don't want to make this about me when you must be struggling to process everything yourself. But it just feels like…"

"Feels like what?" he asks gently.

"Like my fairy-tale love story has been shattered," I admit, wincing at how the words sound said out loud. "And I know how immature that sounds."

"It doesn't," he assures me, kissing the top of my head. "You have every right to feel that way. But a few months from now we might look back at this and see it was just a ploy to try to make us as miserable as she is."

"Or you could be holding your newborn child," I remind him that there is another option. People have sex and get pregnant. No protection is one hundred percent. She could be telling the truth. Or she could be pregnant with someone else's child. Who knows?

Either way, the truth will eventually come out.

We just need to try to hold on for the time being.

I'd hate to walk away from him because it's all too much, and down the line find out she was lying.

Why is life suddenly so hard?

"We don't know how it's going to turn out, I just need to know that no matter what happens, you'll be by my side. I love you, Corey. I know that it's just early days with us, so it's probably easy for you to walk away right now, but I don't want you to. And maybe that makes me selfish, I don't know. But I need you."

I rest my cheek on his shoulder, and we both comfort each other. I need some time to think and clear my head, but I don't see myself leaving him because of something that he didn't choose. Yes, he slept with her, and that's on him, and if it is his child, I need to be able to accept that fact, and that he will be a father. I know he will be a wonderful one, no matter the situation. Maybe Melinda knew that, too.

We stay like that for a while, talking it over, and decide that there's nothing we can do right now until we know for sure.

What can we do?

Torture ourselves with the hypotheticals or try to not let it ruin us.

Damon joins the men and I stay in bed for a while, overthinking and feeling sorry for myself. Pathetic, I know. But I'm going to give myself today to feel all my emotions, before I put my big-girl panties back on to face the day tomorrow.

After a long, hot shower, I stand naked in the mirror and look back down at my wrists. The temptation is there, to just take a razor and do a few little cuts, to just release all of my pain and stress for the day.

Then I can start fresh tomorrow.

A clean slate.

I open the drawer, but then close it and leave the bathroom.

I'm not going backward anymore, only forward.

Chapter Thirty-One

Damon

I wake up the next morning alone in bed and feeling like absolute shit. Corey didn't want to stay the night with me, which is understandable. I didn't get any sleep, and just stayed up the whole night questioning my life choices.

When my phone rings around six AM, I know something must be up. "Yeah?"

"Look out front."

I jump out of bed and open my blinds. "Fuck. I'll be out in a second."

Outside our closed gates is Gio.

On foot, which is weird as hell.

After getting ready quickly, I head outside. Romeo is standing there with Jag and Jeremiah. We all stand back while Romeo walks up to talk to him.

Jag is looking at his phone, where he can check the security footage of our whole property. He's making sure that no one else is around, and that this isn't some kind of planned attack.

"Nothing?" I ask.

"Nope, looks like it's just him. He parked his bike down the road and walked up."

Gio and our Romeo have a quick chat, and then our president returns to us.

"What did he say?" I ask, looking over his shoulder to watch Gio retreat.

"He wants Tatum back, unharmed. He knew we had him," he says, a smirk playing on his lips. "He said they're just here because Tatum wanted to get revenge on the man who murdered his father."

He seems pretty confident that River killed Robert. And although River has never spoken about it, I kind of agree with him. But Bella told me there is no evidence to tie River to anything, and if there was, he'd already be behind bars.

You have to kind of feel bad for the guy. He knows River did it but can't prove anything. And maybe because his father abandoned him, he feels even more like he has to prove himself. Another example of how much of a hold parents have on their children, even when they are grown adults.

"What did you tell him?" Jeremiah asks, while Jag still has his eyes on his phone.

"I told him they can leave first, and then we will let Tatum go," Romeo explains, but his smug expression makes me think his plan goes a little further than that. "He said they'd be out by tomorrow. But if Tatum isn't healthy and alive, he's going to come back and start a war."

I guess the perk about them accusing River of killing Robert is that they know he's not one to mess around with.

And they should be scared.

River is unpredictable and has no qualms hurting people. And he's clearly good at hiding the evidence. I was wondering if he'd be unable to treat Tatum like he would any other enemy, because of his family ties to Corey, but I suppose River is protecting her by handling him. And like she says, Tatum isn't her family. He is nothing to them, and his actions here have proved that.

"What's going to stop them coming back as soon as they have him?" I ask.

"River is working on it," he replies, and I'm guessing he's trying to get some information we can use against them, something that will make them never want to return. "I'll let you all know when we do."

"They wanted him unharmed?"

Romeo laughs. "Yeah, I told Gio that Tatum would be alive, but I don't know about unharmed. He looked very upset about that fact."

Which is a little odd.

Everyone knows you should use your poker face in these situations, but I guess Tatum must be a very close friend to him. Or are they family? That might be something to look into.

Romeo keeps everyone in lockdown, so I head

back to my bedroom and check my phone, hoping to see a text from Corey. Instead, there's one from someone I'd like to never see again.

Melinda: I've made an appointment for next month.

Damon: Okay, send me the details and I'll be there.

I find it weird that she's made it for a month's time. Wouldn't she be about two months by then? Can she know for sure she is pregnant at one month? It seems very early.

Damon: How far along are you?

Melinda: I don't know. When's the last time we had sex? We'll see what the doctor says.

Yes, we will. Finding out how far along she is will be very telling indeed. But she also could have been sleeping with other men around the same time as me, so you never know.

I don't want to be stuck co-parenting with her for the rest of my life, so I'm just hoping this is all some trap.

A trap that I'm going to get out of.

I send Corey a quick text.

Damon: Good morning. I miss you. Can I come there and stay with you?

Corey: Good morning. I think I'm just going to hang out with Bella today. Romeo texted saying we can't leave, so I'm just going to chill here.

She's pushing me away, and I don't know how to fix it.

How does one fix this situation?

A bouquet of flowers and chocolates just aren't going to cut it this time.

There is no "sorry I potentially knocked up a woman just before finally admitting to myself that I was crazy about you but was fighting it" gift out there.

I was putting everything on her, but now it's me who has fucked this up.

My dick should have stayed in its pants.

Damon: If you want time, that's okay, of course I'll give you that, but you can't hide from me forever.

That's a lie. I mean, I'll give her a day, maybe two max, before I go after her and fight for her to forgive me. It's way too early for us to be out of our honeymoon stage. We should have had another year of bliss, at least.

Corey: I'm not hiding from you. Just processing everything.

Damon: Okay, I love you.

Corey: Love you, too.

Sighing, I head to the gym in our clubhouse to punch some shit.

How do things go from amazing to fucked so quickly?

Chapter Thirty-Two

Corey

"Don't you think they are leaving a little too easy?" I ask Leif, who has no choice but to sit on the couch and listen to me vent ever since I shot him. The poor man's suffering is eternal. I even have my sad playlist going on in the background, so he has to listen to all my emotional ballads. "Jealous" by Labrinth is currently playing.

"Yeah, I do," he replies, shrugging. "But they have also heard about River's...reputation, and they know he has Tatum, so if I was them I'd be pretty concerned as well."

"Do they still think you're their insider?" I ask. I'm trying to let myself relax, but I don't know if everything is over yet. My nervous system is still locked in fight or flight.

"Yeah. I think being shot made them trust me

even more, because why would I be loyal to a club that shot me?"

I wince and look over at him. "I'm sorry. You know that, right?"

He smirks. "Well, it's the first time you've said it. But it's fine—it's not the first time I've been shot, and I'm sure it's not going to be the last."

"That's kind of depressing."

"Kind of like this music," he comments.

I ignore it. "You don't have any tattoos?"

He shakes his head. "Nope, too much of a commitment."

"I see."

"So do you want to keep discussing everything except Damon and his new baby mama?" he asks, studying me.

"Yes. Who braids your hair?" I deflect once more.

He laughs. "I have a lady."

"Do you, now?"

"Just for my hair, yes, I do," he replies, eyes going back to the TV screen, where *Shameless* is playing.

Blaze walks in and sits down next to me. "What's with the pornstache?" I ask.

Leif laughs, probably thrilled that it's no longer him getting grilled.

Blaze stokes the hairy caterpillar in question. It makes him look like he's contemplating life. "Believe it or not, women like it. And more importantly, I like it."

"I like your self-confidence."

"I like your red hair," he replies, reaching out and touching a curly strand. "There's a lot of it."

"Indeed. You guys are all right, you know that? I didn't know what it would be like having new randoms around here, but I'm quite enjoying it," I say, smiling as I reach for my phone, seeing if Damon had messaged me again.

Bella joins us with some snacks, and I know she's missing my brother while he's away torturing my other brother. Wow, there's a sentence I never thought I'd be saying. "Thank you," I say, grabbing a handful of popcorn.

"Of course," she replies, snuggling in next to me.

Julianna pops her head around the corner. "Damon's here."

I share a look with Bella. He said he was going to give me time. It's been two days.

Blaze laughs and slides as far away from me as he can without falling off the couch. "We're an impatient type of male."

"Clearly," I mutter, getting up so the whole room doesn't hear whatever Damon is about to say to me.

And there he is, walking in with Romeo, his gray eyes like angry clouds, going straight to me.

"Hey," he says, coming up to me, while Romeo keeps on walking. "I know I said I'd give you time, but I'm going crazy just sitting at home thinking of you being here upset and angry at me."

I smile sadly and go closer to him, resting my cheek on his chest, while his strong arms come around me. "I'm glad you came," I admit, sighing. I know that's probably giving him mixed signals, but now that he's here I feel a bit better. We go into my room for some privacy and end up snuggled together on the bed.

"Whatever happens, I don't want it to break us up," he says, stroking my back. "And I know that's easier for me to say than you, because it's me needing the support and you who is going to have to deal with all the shit that comes with this situation. But I can't lose you. I only just got you."

He's right, it *will* be me having to compromise and be put in a less-than-ideal situation.

But it is what it is. I have two options. I either walk away, or I agree to stay and whatever happens, I make it work for him, and support him through it all.

If I do the former, I could have major regrets. I'd miss him so much, and I'd have to watch him move on with his life. And the baby might not even be his. With the latter, it's not going to be an easy ride. He could potentially have to co-parent with Melinda and be tied to her for the rest of his life, and I wouldn't be giving him his firstborn child, which is kind of a hard pill to swallow if I'm being completely honest. Even if I'm unsure whether I want children in the first place, which makes the whole thing even more confusing.

But I think I've always known what I'm going to do.

Now, if he had cheated on me and gotten her pregnant, this would be a completely different outcome. I would have been out of here the second Melinda got out of that car. But we weren't together then, and although I don't like it one bit, he was free to be with whoever he wanted.

"We'll get through this," I tell him, lifting my head up to look at him. "Somehow."

He smiles and gently pushes my hair off my face. "I'm so sorry you have to go through this. And that I ruined our fairy tale."

"I guess no relationship is perfect," I reply. "You're just going to have to be an extra-fucking-amazing boyfriend."

He kisses my forehead. "Now, that I can do."

With all of our personal shit taking up all of my time and focus, I almost forget about everything else going on in our lives.

But I guess I'm easily reminded when Romeo rushes into my room without even knocking.

"They must have tracked us somehow," he says, and I quickly get off Damon, who jumps off the bed.

"Go to Julianna," he says, gently pushing me out before him. "Stay with her and Bella."

I find them in the nursery, and I stare up at the wall mural I painted for Julian when he was born.

"I thought they said they're going to leave," I say in a whisper-yell. "What are they doing back here?" Like I needed any more drama today.

"I guess they didn't like the offer we made," Julianna replies, sitting in her rocking chair with

Julian. "There's almost no chance they can get in here, though, but if they do, we need to go to the basement."

"That's where all the weapons are, too," I add, my mind already concocting a plan in case it all goes to hell. "What about Leif? He's injured—should we bring him in here with us?"

"I'm sure he'll be fine," Bella assures me, opening the curtains to look out the window. "He's a Viking."

Yes, yes, he is.

All I know is that if I hear them getting through the gates and onto the property, I'm going to the basement.

To get a gun.

Leif hobbles into the room on his crutches. "Gio must be getting desperate. He's asked me to kill River's old lady in retaliation. He wants me to do it as soon as they let Tatum free."

We all look at Bella, who gasps. "You aren't going to, right?"

Leif simply grins. "No, I like my balls where they are."

"Smart," I mutter.

Chapter Thirty-Three

Damon

This time it's Gio and all of his men at the gate, motorcycles rumbling.

We're all packing and ready to fight if it comes to that, and I know they are, too. All I know is that they're not making it inside that clubhouse, not with the women in there.

But Gio surprises us.

"We're leaving now!" he calls out, looking out at all of us. "We are keeping our end of the deal, and now you better keep yours."

"We will," Romeo replies, placing his hand on his chest. "You have my word."

They all rumble off into the night, hopefully to never fucking return, but I don't think we are that lucky.

An hour or so later, we get yet another unexpected

guest at our front gate. The gate that we used to just leave open but is now permanently locked.

"What are you doing here?" Romeo asks, scowling.

Rosalind is Romeo's Melinda.

I think every man has one. And somehow knowing that brings me a little comfort.

Rosalind crosses her arms and stares him down. Her eyes going to mine, back to Romeo. She's sitting in her car, wearing crystal necklaces and rings that must have come from her new store. "Let me in. I have information."

He opens the gate and lets her in, but tells her to stay in the car. "What do you want, Rosalind? Bored now that Gio's left?"

She purses her pink glossy lips and leans out the window. "Look, I know you guys don't like me, and I know I've done some shitty things in the name of revenge, but I would never let anything happen to my nephew."

"You haven't even met your nephew," Romeo points out.

She hesitates, then admits, "Mom and Dad let me see him when they babysat him the other weekend."

Shit.

Julianna is going to be pissed.

"And I know you're going to be angry, but he's the sweetest little boy, and he's just a child. I would never let anything happen to him," she continues, looking toward the clubhouse door.

"Well, that won't be happening again, unless Julianna approves of it," Romeo replies, his voice icy cold. "And what's going on with you and the Lost Lions MC?"

"Yes, I partied with them. So what? None of the bikers here will go near me now after what I did. And I deserve a little fun, too."

"So why are you here?" I ask, scowling. "You have no loyalty to us, and we don't have any for you, except for the fact that you are Julianna's sister and Paulie's daughter. It's a shame you don't have their good character."

She turns her cold eyes to me. "Nice to see you too, Damon. And if the two of you stop having a go at me, you can hear what I came to say. I know what the Lost Lions MC is planning on doing next. I overheard Gio speaking with his sergeant at arms when I was at their place."

"I wish we could trust what you say, Rosalind. But unfortunately you've lost your credibility here. For all we know you coming here right now is part of their plan," Romeo says to her, crossing his arms over his chest.

"Well, I heard him say that he has an insider here, one of your new prospects, and he has asked him to kill Bella the second Tatum is released," she says, looking between us. "I'm sure that information would be of use to you."

This has us both intrigued, because obviously Gio thinks it's true about Leif. So, her information is right—we just already know it. River was fucking pissed when he learned about it, and we're grateful that Leif is loyal to us.

"And what else?" Romeo presses, and she smirks, knowing she now has his interest.

"They are going to get Tatum, then go to River's mom Lisa's house to kill her. Which was his original plan, but you guys obviously stopped him. He also wanted Leif to set the clubhouse on fire on his way out, and then meet them a few towns over."

"I hope you're being honest for once in your life, Rosalind," he says.

A flash of sadness and regret appears in her eyes. "I am. I promise. I don't want Julian caught up in this bullshit—he doesn't deserve any of it."

I don't know why she has this sudden love for her nephew, but she's been asking to see him since he was born. And now she finally has. Maybe she does have a soft spot for him, even though she doesn't have the same feeling for her sister.

"Okay, then. Thank you for letting us know."

"You're welcome," she replies, and then backs out of the driveway.

Romeo turns to me, his hand on my shoulder, head lowered. "What do you think? She was right about Leif—what if she's right about the rest? Or is she setting us up for a trap? They could all be waiting at Lisa's house for us. Or on the road along the way."

I realize that without River here, I have become

Romeo's second most trusted, his right-hand man, and I'm proud to be given that position.

"We need to get their mom to the clubhouse," I tell him, because it's not worth the risk. "What's the best way to do that? Would she get in her car and drive here? Less conspicuous than a group of motorcycles."

"We need her here before River lets Tatum go," he says, pulling out his phone. "Get Corey to call her mom and tell her she needs to come here now. Otherwise, we need to leave right now to go and get her."

Shit.

I don't know how it's going to go with Corey's mom here, especially after how upset she was with her. Still, I guess it doesn't matter. If Rosalind isn't being a treacherous liar, they are going to kill her in revenge.

And we can't let that happen.

Chapter Thirty-Four

Corey

When Damon tells me what Rosalind said, I feel a whole bunch of different emotions. One, I don't want my mother hurt, so of course I want to do whatever we need to save her. Two, I don't want her here, with me. Three, I also don't trust Rosalind as far as I can carry her, which is a big "not at all."

But that doesn't matter right now.

I call Mom's number, and she finally picks up on the tenth ring. "Mom? It's Corey. Listen to me: you aren't safe, there are men coming to your house. Can you drive to us? Or do you want us to come and pick you up?"

She sighs on the other end. "I will be fine. I told you, Tatum won't hurt me."

I grit my teeth and hand the phone to Romeo. Who tells her the exact same thing, except this time, of course, she agrees to get in her car and drive here.

I don't know how she continues to make me feel so small with any interaction I have with her.

But here I am, still not good enough.

Romeo kisses the top of my head. "It's not you, it's her."

I look up at him. "She makes me feel like it's me. I know she basically raised you, so you care about her, but I don't get that same version of her."

"She's different now," he admits, brown eyes gentle. "Especially after Matthew died. Don't take anything she says or does personally, Corey. She has her own issues and I think since you're her only daughter, she takes them out on you."

"She needs to go to therapy."

He laughs, and scruffs my hair. "Yes, she does. But right now, we just want to keep her alive so that River doesn't kill us."

"Fair enough."

Julianna comes into the kitchen, face red with anger. "I can't believe my parents let Rosalind be around Julian. I specifically told them not to! They are never looking after him again because they clearly don't respect my boundaries. I just can't trust her, and I wish that I could. But after everything she's just not someone I want around him."

I can totally understand where she's coming from. My mom won't be going around any kids that I may or may not have.

I frown as it hits me that I even entertained the thought of having kids for a second.

Shit.

Am I becoming more flexible to the idea?

Who am I?

"It's okay," I say, taking both her hands in mine. "Breathe, Julianna. It won't happen again. And he's fine. Now you know you can't leave him with them without them letting her see him."

She nods, taking deep breaths. "The thought of her holding him makes me feel sick. He's the next president of this MC, the MC that she betrayed! All because she didn't get the guy she wanted."

I nod, letting her vent.

"Would you turn against us if you didn't get Damon?" she asks, but answers for me anyway. "No, you would not! Because you are a loyal, beautiful person."

"I'd probably just go for one of the prospects instead," I whisper, and she laughs, the tension leaving her body.

"Out of curiosity, which one?" she asks, lowering her tone.

"I don't know, because I haven't been looking at them like that because I'm head over heels for Damon," I reply, glancing out to make sure no one else can hear this hypothetical conversation we're having right now, right in the middle of a crisis, might I add. "But going on looks alone, I think Blaze. The boxing thing is hot, and goddamn but that pornstache is growing on me."

She bursts out laughing, then covers her mouth

before someone comes in to ask what's so funny. "Okay, I'm never going to repeat that."

"Excuse me, how about you? Who would you pick if Romeo didn't exist?"

She just laughs and leaves the kitchen.

Sneaky.

Damon comes in when I'm squatting down in the fridge, trying to find the snacks I hid in here last night.

"If you're looking for the chocolate-covered strawberries, Jag found them," he says, running his hands over my ass.

"There is no time for that right now," I reply in a dry tone, standing back up and closing the fridge with a swing of my hip. "My mother is on her way here now. Are you ready to meet her? You're probably more ready than I am."

"Are you going to tell her about us?" he asks, pinning me back against the fridge door. "Or are you going to save that for another time?"

"I have nothing to hide," I reply, my gaze dropping to his lips. "But she'll probably have something to say. She might ask you why you want to be with me, or something like that. Who knows?"

"And I'll tell her it's because you are the most beautiful," he stops to kiss me, "Sexy," another kiss. "Intelligent," another kiss, "talented woman I've ever met in my life. I'd be a fool to let that go."

"You *would* be a fool," I agree, grabbing onto his face and kissing him back.

"Yes, get that all out of your system before your mom comes here," Bella teases, amusement in her tone.

I look around Damon to see her. "Great, I forgot that you've met my mom, and that she loves you. That makes it all so much worse." I bet Bella is the daughter she always wanted, but never had. Just another slap in the face.

"It will be fine, Corey. I promise you. We all have your back."

"I know. Now if you will excuse me, I'm going to go and mentally prepare myself for seeing her after all of this time," I say, gently pushing Damon off me and making an escape to my bedroom. He gives me about half an hour before he comes to check on me.

"You okay?" he asks, closing the door behind him. "She's going to be here soon. You know if you don't want to see her, we can just hide up here for a while?"

He wanders around my room, looking at my art, until he comes across the easel in the far corner. When I hear his slight gasp, I lift my head up to see what he's looking at.

Ah, shit.

"When did you do this?" he asks, raising it up into the sunlight and examining it. "Corey, this is amazing. Why didn't you show me?"

Sitting up, I enjoy watching his expression as he stares at the painting of himself. I spent extra time trying to get the color of his eyes just right, the close-up portrait showing every perfect angle of his face.

"I painted it before we were together. And then I forgot about it. Or maybe I hid it, because it's kind of embarrassing to be painting a man that wasn't even mine."

"Well, I'm yours now, and I don't think it's embarrassing at all. It's beautiful."

"You've always been my muse, Damon. Ever since I first laid eyes on you."

I could paint him all day. I wish he knew how truly beautiful he is to me, inside and out. Whatever life throws at us, he's worth it.

He holds up the painting next to his face. "I think you've made me better-looking than I am in real life. See, love really is blind."

I roll my eyes. "Modesty doesn't look good on you. The painting pales in comparison to you. You are seriously the hottest man I've ever seen in real life."

"Yes, blind," he replies, with a cheeky smile. "Can I hang this up in my bedroom? This is the best thing I've ever seen. It shouldn't be hidden away in the corner of your room."

"Sure, you can have it," I reply, laughing at the best thing he's ever seen being a painting of his own face. "It was always meant to be yours."

He puts it down and jumps on the bed, cuddling up against me. "When this is over, I'm taking you on a date. A proper date."

"I'd like that, and maybe afterward you can rip off my clothes…"

A knock on my door makes me jump. "Lisa just called. She will be here in thirty," Julianna calls out.

Wonderful.

"I guess we better get this over with, then," I sigh, looking up at the ceiling. "At least she's safe, right? I'm going to keep saying that to myself over and over again."

Maybe she will surprise me and be kind and hug me. And tell me she has missed me? I can dream. I've pushed her out of my mind as much as I can, and that's how I've been dealing with it, but now there's no more hiding.

I don't need her to like me.

I don't need her to like me.

I am a good person.

Damon kisses my temple and helps me get up. "Don't let anything she says get to you, okay? Don't let anyone have that power over you, even your own mother. You know who you are. Everyone who loves you knows who you are. And that is enough."

It is enough.

And I am enough.

Chapter Thirty-Five

Damon

The fact that Corey's such a mess over seeing her own mother makes me feel sick to my stomach. Why can't this woman just love her child? How hard is it? I've never met Lisa before, but the things I've heard I don't like.

I'm just going to be there for Corey and try to keep everyone calm. My getting angry on her behalf won't help the situation, it would likely escalate it, but I will stand up for her if her mom is too out of line. No one talks down to my woman. I don't care who it is.

When Lisa arrives, Romeo helps her out of her car and ushers her inside. She looks more like River than Corey, but I can see some of Corey in her through her facial expressions.

"Everyone, this is River and Corey's mom, Lisa. She will be staying with us for a few days. Bella set you up in one of our guest rooms," he says, leading her through the clubhouse.

"Where is River?" she asks.

"He's, uuhhh, out on business," Romeo answers, and the two of them stop when they see Corey and me.

With my hand on the small of Corey's back, we both greet her. "Hi, Mom," Corey says.

Lisa, who has a patch covering one eye, turns to her daughter. "Corey," she says, in a curt tone, then looks over at me. "And who do we have here?"

"I'm Damon," I say, offering her my hand.

She shakes it, while looking between me and her daughter. "And you are her boyfriend?"

"Yes, he is," Corey says, sparing me a quick glance.

"I see," she replies, her visible eye giving me a once-over. "You are a very handsome man."

"Thank you," I reply, and she nods and keeps walking.

That's it.

A compliment to me, and not even a hug for her daughter. I look down at Corey and watch her as she sees Bella approach and Lisa embrace her warmly. Like a daughter. And I know her heart must be breaking. I bring her against me and kiss her forehead. She melts into me and flashes me a sad smile, before we follow everyone into the kitchen, where Bella is laying out some food for everyone.

"I don't understand why Tatum would want to hurt me," Lisa is saying to Romeo.

"He wants revenge on River," he explains, sitting down next to her. "And you live out there by yourself, so he came up with the idea of going after you."

"I've never really had much to do with him," she says, thanking Bella when she hands her a mug of coffee. "He lived with his mother, and Robert rarely saw him. He always said he was a mistake. I thought it was his business if he wanted a relationship with his firstborn, not mine. He never made the effort. And then years passed, and I saw Tatum at his funeral, and that's it. Why does he want revenge against River?"

Does she actually not know that River killed her husband?

She must.

"He's joined another motorcycle club, which we are having issues with," is all Romeo says back to her, clearly uncomfortable with the question. And fair enough, because how could she not know?

"Wow, okay," she mutters, absently touching her eye patch. "How long do you think I'll have to stay here for? I have animals I've left at home. The neighbors can feed them for now, but I'd like to go home as soon as I can."

"I'm not sure. A couple days at most, hopefully," he replies, looking over at Corey. "Maybe you could spend some time with Corey while you're here."

Lisa gazes at her daughter. "Yes, well, I guess we will both be stuck here until the threat is gone."

The vibe in the house is definitely different with

her here, with more tension filling the room. Romeo asks Corey to show her to her room so Lisa knows where she is staying, and Corey takes her down the hall. I stay in the kitchen to give them some time alone, although that might not be the best idea.

"She's very cold to her," Bella whispers, frowning with concern in her gray eyes. "I know River said they have a strained relationship, but that was awkward to be around."

"I know. I don't know why she's like that with her, but nice to everyone else around her. She can't seriously blame her for Matthew's death? She had nothing to do with it," I say, deciding to follow her to make sure that she's okay.

I stop at the door as I hear Lisa's words. "Are you pregnant? How did you get a man like that?"

My jaw clenches hard at her cruel words.

"No, I'm not pregnant, Mom," Corey replies, sighing. "I don't even know if I want kids. Damon loves me for who I am."

Lisa makes a scoffing sound. "You don't want children? I suppose that's probably a good thing."

The anger that fills me is second to none. How dare she speak to Corey like that? Sweet, beautiful Corey, who is so kind to everyone.

"Why do you hate me so much?" Corey blurts out, and I know it must have taken her a lot to ask that.

"I don't hate you, Corey. But it's just hard to look at you when I think about Matthew. He died protecting you. I can't help but think if you had just stayed home that night, maybe he would still be here. I miss my son every day."

"I miss him, too! And it wasn't my fault he died—he was in an MC, and there are risks with that. Which is why you're here right now! I wish I could redo that day, but I can't, and I don't think it's fair that you blame me for his death. I didn't kill him. I would have done anything to protect him," she says, and the pain and emotion in her voice makes me want to run to her and save her from this conversation. But unfortunately, this is one that needs to be had.

"I know! I know," Lisa replies, her voice breaking. "And I do love you, Corey. You are my only daughter. But sometimes I wish it was you who died instead of Matthew."

And that is my limit.

I step inside the room and go to Corey, who is silently crying, big, fat tears dripping down her cheeks.

"You don't get to speak to her like that," I say, keeping my tone even. Underneath, though, I'm seeing red. "And you should be ashamed by speaking to your child like that. She has done nothing wrong and deserves the same love you give your other children. What, are you one of those moms who sees their daughter as competition or something? I don't get it. Corey is beautiful, smart, and funny. And she loves everyone around her so hard. I couldn't have dreamed up a better woman if I tried."

Lisa looks down but says nothing.

I grab Corey and drag her out of there.

I have never met a more toxic, heartless woman in my life.

When we get to our bedroom, it hits me that she might be upset that I got involved and spoke to her mother like that. I really tried to stay out of it but hearing her say those things really set me off. No wonder Corey has struggled in the past with her mental health and feeling lost in life.

"I'm sorry," I say when the door locks. "I shouldn't have said that to your mom. I just couldn't stand by and let her speak to you like that—"

She shuts me up with a kiss. "Thank you. No one has defended me like that before, especially not to her. She's not like that with River, so he doesn't understand how awful she is to me."

I sigh in relief that she's not angry about it. "I just couldn't hear any more of what she was saying. It wasn't true. And I know I shouldn't have been eavesdropping, but I had a feeling she was going to piss me off and say something to hurt you, and she fucking did."

Corey kisses me again. "I love you."

"I love you, too."

And I'm not going to let anyone, even her own mother, ever hurt her again.

Chapter Thirty-Six

Corey

Damon telling my mom off must have gotten me a little hot, because we end up fucking against my door, his hard cock pushing me back against the wood with each thrust.

I don't care who hears. I don't care what my mom thinks. I think it's time I let that all go because I can't control her actions. And Damon is right, I don't deserve any of the shit she dishes out to me. I don't need to be around her and her toxic opinions. She's my mother, she should have those parent goggles that other parents have. Most parents think their kids can't do anything wrong, and everything they do is perfect. They brag about their kids' mediocre abilities, but mine can't even look me in the eye anymore.

Romeo was correct—it is her, not me.

And I can't fix her. She needs to fix herself.

But she won't.

So, I'll forever be the black sheep, and I'm going to have to learn to accept that and be okay with it.

Mom is in the lounge room watching a movie with Romeo, Julianna, and Julian when we go back downstairs, so I give that area wide berth and head outside, where Bella is on her phone, furiously texting.

"Hey," I say, sitting down next to her.

She turns to me. "Hey, are you okay? I'm so sorry about your mom. I'm actually shocked at how mean she is to you. I was just messaging River about it. I'm so angry he hasn't handled this."

"Well, we haven't seen each other in a long time, so River hasn't had to really be around her when I'm there," I reply, looking out over the yard. "And she's not like this with him. It is what it is, I suppose. Damon had words with her, and now I think I'm just going to avoid her until it's time for her to leave."

"Fair enough. I wouldn't want to be around that, either," she admits, turning and lifting her legs so they are resting on my lap. "It's a miracle you turned out so well, Corey. You should be proud of yourself. You've grown so much since I first met you, too. I'm so happy you are my sister."

Swallowing hard, I nod in agreement. "I'm happy you are, too."

Even though it's hard to see Mom be to kind and loving to Bella, it would be worse to see her be rude and cold to Bella.

I wouldn't wish it on anyone else.

It is my burden to bear.

"River said he got what he needed from Tatum, so he's releasing him to Gio now," she says, reading her phone screen.

"Hopefully this is all going to be over soon," I mutter, wanting today to end. It's been a long day. "What do you think about Rosalind? Think she was on our side?"

"I don't know, she's a bit of a wild card, isn't she? I mean, she knew about Leif, and if he wasn't on our side that information could have potentially saved my life."

"That's true."

If Leif wasn't loyal to us, Bella could be dead right now, and our clubhouse would have been on fire. Lucky for us, though, we were one step ahead of the Lost Lions MC.

"Maybe she really does care for Julian. He's pretty cute—how could anyone not?"

"Yeah, maybe. I hope she's trying to redeem herself, but who knows? I'm just ready for life to go back to normal. Lisa can go back home, River can return, and we can walk around town doing whatever we want again. I'm never taking my freedom for granted again," she says, pointing up to the sky. "Look, it's a butterfly."

And what do you know, it comes and lands right on me. "Every time I see a big, blue butterfly I think it's Matthew," I admit, and she smiles warmly. "You're not mad I'm giving up on Mom, are you?"

I ask the butterfly. "I hope you're not, but I need to focus on me now."

"I think he agrees with you," Bella comments quietly. "We all do."

He flies away, and I stare after him longingly.

And in this moment, I forgive myself, and let go of any guilt I've been holding over his death.

It wasn't my fault, and if I could have, I would have died instead.

But I'm here, and that must be for a reason. I'm going to live and enjoy my life without feeling like I don't deserve to.

Closing my eyes, I take it all in, and feel everything, all the pain, and regret, and grief and then let it all go.

The only person I need to love me is myself.

"By the way, we could all hear you guys having sex up there," Bella says casually, ruining my peaceful moment as she tries to hide her laughter. "I'm glad River wasn't here."

"Me, too." I smirk.

But it was worth it.

Old me would have gone into my room and hidden for the rest of the day, but I'm not going anywhere. Yes, I have hot sex with my man, just like every other couple here.

And I don't care.

"But I'm a woman with needs, and this time it couldn't wait."

I needed him inside of me for my sanity, for my soul.

It was a soul fuck.

"No judgment here." She grins, turning to face me. "You know, I remember Damon once came into the office and asked me about you. He was trying to get any information he could out of me, and I tried to tell him without telling him that it was probably a bad idea and that he should leave you alone. I'm so glad he didn't listen to me—you two are a perfect match for each other, and you haven't let River, the age difference, or a potential baby mama break you up."

"We really have been through a lot in a short time," I reply, wrinkling my nose. "It fast-tracks a relationship, though, doesn't it? And you're right, I have done a lot of growing in that time."

"You have."

Romeo comes out to check on us, and he looks stressed, his hair all mussed and dark circles under his eyes. "Tatum is back with his MC, and River is on his way home. Hopefully by tomorrow night, they will be out of our town."

If Leif were a traitor, now would be the time he'd be targeting Bella. It's a terrifying thought.

"What's to stop them from coming back?" I ask, and Romeo simply grins.

"River found out a few things I don't think they will want getting out. We aren't opposed to a little blackmail. We also found out that Tatum has a son, and he lives here in Vegas. I don't know if Tatum's like his own father and wouldn't care, but we want him to know that we know." He puts his hands up. "Stop looking at me like that. I'd never harm a child. But the threat will hopefully be enough for him."

"I have a nephew?" I ask, sitting up straighter.

"Yes, you do. He's five years old."

I sit back and process yet another surprise. I hope the child is doing okay. Depending on what the mother is like, maybe she would let me see him? Or is that a bad idea?

I can't imagine it would be safe trying to go and find out who the mother is, and I don't have anything to do with Tatum, so maybe it's just best that I do nothing.

I can only hope the child is well loved and cared for.

River returns home and Bella runs into his arms. He's been off torturing our enemy, and she still loves him and thinks he is the perfect man. If that isn't true love, I don't know what is.

"Corey." He smiles, hugging me and lifting me off the ground. "Nice to see you, sister."

"You too, I'm glad you made it back safe. I thought maybe they'd be hiding in the bushes waiting to ambush you or something."

He smirks. "They can try. Where's Mom?"

"In the lounge," I say, leaving it at that. He goes to find her, and to greet the rest of the MC. He seems awfully refreshed, which is a little concerning.

We all have a barbecue that night and pretend like this whole week hasn't been one fucking disaster.

And I like it that way.

Chapter Thirty-Seven

Damon

As I look down at the blackmail they have on Tatum and Gio, my eyes widen as I slide the photographs away. "All of this and you also somehow got the cops on our side? How did you manage that one?"

"They don't want the Lost Lions MC around here, causing trouble. They barely like having us around here, you know that. Better the known devil, right? They said they will arrest them the second they ever return. If they are stupid enough to do so," Romeo replies.

"Arrest them on what grounds?" I ask, looking around the table. Romeo called a meeting this morning, and for once included the women, too, so we're all here to debrief everything that has happened with the Lost Lions MC and how we are going to protect ourselves going forward.

"Drug possession." Romeo grins.

And I'm guessing that will happen whether or not they actually have drugs on them. I know a few cops from our local police department wouldn't be above planting some to get what they want.

"They have left, we had a confirmed sighting of them a few towns over," River adds. "They took Tatum to a hospital there."

I don't know what River did to him exactly, but I can guess, and it isn't pretty.

"I'll be escorting my mom home today and checking if they trashed her house or if they went there looking for her," he adds, looking over at me. "I know Corey has had a hard time with her here, and it will be better when she's gone."

I nod, agreeing with him. "I think that's for the best."

"She was awful," Julianna adds.

"I'm sorry," River says as he turns to Corey. "I should have protected you from her all these years. I didn't realize…"

"It's not on you," she replies. "It's her."

"River, take a couple of men with you just in case," Romeo orders. "Lockdown is over, but just be careful, because we don't know if they left any other surprises for us other than Leif taking us down." He turns to him. "Thank you for not torching our home."

Leif's lip twitches. "Anytime, guys."

I take Corey out for lunch afterward, and we enjoy being out and about, and alone.

"You glad your mom is gone?" I ask, already knowing the answer.

She dips her fry into aioli sauce and nods. "Yeah, it's sad but I am. She did come and say bye and gave me a small hug, so maybe she felt bad after what you said to her. I don't think she's been called out on it like that before, so hopefully she thinks about it and realizes that what she does is wrong. I doubt it, but a woman can hope."

"I guess you can't change some people and the way they see things, even if it's all misconstrued," I say, watching as she takes a bite of her steak.

"This is so good, thank you for taking me out, it's exactly what I need."

"Me, too," I admit, enjoying my beer. "This week has been extremely stressful, and we still have to watch our back in case these assholes decide to be bold."

"I wonder what River will find when he goes to Mom's house. If they did try to go there to get her, Rosalind was right, and we probably should say thank you to her," Corey points out, wincing at the thought. "I mean, I know she kidnapped me and all, but maybe if we show some appreciation, she can let go of her villain era and turn her life around."

"I think her issues are more than just a villain era."

"True. She did have the shred of decency to tell us, although she could have had ulterior motives for that. Maybe they did something to piss her off, so she wanted to get back at them, who knows."

We finish our lunch, and then I put her on the back of my bike and take her for a long ride, until we reach this beautiful two-story property by the lake.

She looks up at the house as she gets off the bike. "Are we going to the beach? Why did you park here? Wow, this house is insane."

I hide my smile. "Do you like it? I wanted you to have a look at it before I bought it."

She turns to me, confused. "What?"

"Yeah, I thought it might be nice for us to have our own place so we can get some privacy." I lower my lips to her ear. "A place where you can scream as loud as you want."

Her eyes widen, and she turns to look at the house again. "You want to buy us a sex pad?"

"I want to buy us a property, so one day we can move in here together. We can't live at the clubhouse forever. Look at all the original members—they all have their own homes now to raise their families," I say, looking up at the balcony I wouldn't mind fucking her on. "And if that family is just me, you, and a few dogs, I'm okay with that, too."

"Really?" she asks, her brow furrowing. "You'd really be okay if we didn't have any children together? I mean, you might be having one without me, of course."

"I'm happy with whatever makes you happy, and if you don't want children, I will accept that. We can live our best selfish lives forever," I say, and she laughs.

"Down the line, maybe I will feel a different way," she says, surprising me. "I never wanted kids, but with you, I don't know. I'm not shutting it down completely."

"Okay, well, we will leave it open, with both of us willing to see how it goes," I say, opening the gate door for her. "And let's have a look inside and see what you think. If you like it, it's yours. If not, we can find something else."

We have a look around. The interior is very modern, spacious, and extremely stylish. I love it, and I hope she does, too. She looks up at the high ceilings, the chandelier, and runs her fingers along the black marble countertop in the kitchen. "Damon, this is beautiful."

"Yeah?"

"Yeah. It's perfect," she says, walking out onto the balcony. "And look at this view, Damon. Wow. I can't believe this is going to be our home!" She turns around with a big smile and jumps into my arms, wrapping her legs around me. "I love it. And I have a lot of money in my bank if you want me to pay for anything, or put in half—"

I stop her right there. "Do I look like a fifty-fifty kind of man? I'm paying for it all, it's yours. I love you, and you deserve it. We deserve it. And I'm going to give you everything you could ever want. And don't ever offer to pay for anything again."

I'm her man—it's my job to provide and look after her. And I will.

I lean her up against the glass sliding door and look into her eyes. "I love you."

"I love you," she replies, her breath hitching.

And then the next second our lips are on each other, and our clothes are coming off, and I'm fucking her against the sliding door, out in the open where anyone on the road could see.

"Yes, Damon," she moans, kissing my neck and grinding against me. She feels so fucking good, and she's so wet. Suddenly I stop when I realize just why she feels so damn good.

"I'm not wearing a condom," I gasp, and she keeps moving against me.

"I don't care. I'm on the pill—don't stop," she says, so I keep fucking her until she comes all over my cock.

And then I bend her over the balcony and fuck her until I do the same, coming in her sweet pussy without protection for the first time.

And fuck, it feels so good.

I wrap my arms around her, breathing heavily, my cock still inside of her.

"Fucking me with a view of the lake, what a way to end a date," she says, and we both start laughing.

And then a car beeps at us, so we get the fuck out of there.

Chapter Thirty-Eight

Corey

Sitting outside in the garden, I lift my brush to the easel, enjoying the sunshine on my face as I process my life right now while I paint. A week has passed with no drama, and it's been heaven. I stay with Damon most nights, and we're in our own little loved-up bubble. River has gotten used to us being together, and he and Damon have been getting along well. So there is that miracle. Life seems to be pretty damn good right now, except for one thing.

Melinda.

I've accepted the fact that Damon might be having a baby. And if it is his, I would love and care for that child the same way I would for my own. Because it's still *his* child, and I love him no matter what.

But we still have to get to the bottom of whether Melinda actually is pregnant. Damon told me how she still hasn't shown him so much as an ultrasound photo, so he's waiting to go to the appointment she set up in a few weeks' time.

Since she sent him that message, though, she's been quiet, which is a little confusing, because I thought she'd be harassing him. I know she asked for money, which makes me wonder if that was her plan all along. But then I feel guilty about judging her. What if she is pregnant with his child, and does need money? I'd say give it to her. Not like we're short on it. But I also don't want him to be taken advantage of. It seems very suspicious, and I don't trust her one bit.

Why is it all so hard?

"What are you thinking about so intently?" Bella asks, coming to sit outside with me while I paint.

"Damon's baby," I admit, dipping my brush in the blue paint. "And whether or not we are being assholes."

"You are not," she assures me, taking a sip of her coffee. Now that things are back to normal, she's back at work as a property manager. While we do have an office here, she usually goes out to have meetings with clients. Today must be one of those days, because she is dressed to business perfection in a black suit, with red lipstick sealing the deal. "When you find out the truth, then you can go from there, but right now you're all in limbo, which sucks."

She stands up and comes over to see what I'm painting. "That's beautiful. I have to go to work now, but I'll see you later this afternoon."

She kisses me on the cheek and leaves.

I stare at the butterfly I've painted. It's flying over the desert, off into the sunset. Looking at it just makes me think of Matthew and smile. I smile wider thinking of how Damon hung the painting of him in his bedroom, and he stops to admire it whenever he walks past.

Over this last week, I've had a lot of time to think about what I want to do in life, and I've decided to go back to college next fall and finish my business degree. As much as I've been enjoying my time off, I'm getting a little antsy now, and want something to challenge me a little more. And with my degree, I can help the MC continue to build their empire and create generational wealth for all the members in the club.

"Am I interrupting your creativity?" Damon asks as he steps outside, holding a plate of snacks.

"No, you are my muse, remember? And what do you have there?" I ask, putting my brush down.

"Well, you always stock the house with everyone's favorite foods, and all the men love you for it. And I love you for being so thoughtful. But today I went and got all *your* favorites and made it into a platter for you," he says, presenting it to me. "And proof that I pay attention to you."

"That is very sweet," I say, eying the carefully picked plate of my all-time-favorite chocolates, fruit, and sweets. "Thank you."

"You're welcome," he says, giving me a kiss.

I touch his leather cut. "You heading out?"

"Yeah, we're going for a ride and then I have to go to Devil's Play."

"That reminds me, I need to text Echo. She wanted to catch up. I should tell her to come over here and she can hang out."

His hands slide down to my hips, and he pulls me in for a kiss. "Sounds good. I'm sure the prospects will enjoy having a single woman around."

"She's not coming for them," I say, arching my brow. "I'll see you later."

"Love you," he says, disappearing back inside. I pull out my phone to text her before I forget.

Corey: Drinks here tomorrow night?

Echo: Perfect! I have work until nine, but I'll come straight there after.

Corey: Great, I'll see you then.

Echo: Want me to bring anything?

Corey: Just yourself.

The next two hours are spent finishing both the platter and the painting, and once I check out the final product, I decide to mail it to my mom instead of keeping it.

She needs some peace in her life.

"Where are you off to?" Jag asks when he sees

me grabbing my keys with my bag slung across my shoulder.

"I thought I'd go to the store and get some food and alcohol for the party I'm throwing tomorrow night," I say, and his eyes light up. "I've invited Echo over. Do you want to invite anyone?"

"Yes, I'd like to invite the good doctor. I don't know if she'll come, but a man can dream."

"She better come, otherwise you aren't doing it right," I joke as I head out the door, closing it on his laughter.

"The good doctor," I mutter to myself in amusement. In all honesty, I'd like to meet this Dr. Shine.

I do a big grocery shop, then get some alcohol and mixers. For my last stop, I walk back into the crystal store, and head to the counter where Rosalind is standing, writing something down in a notebook.

"Hey," I say, as she lifts her head.

"Corey, what do you want?" she asks, studying me through narrowed eyes.

"I just wanted to come in and say thank you for coming to the clubhouse to give us that information. I don't know what made you do it, but I appreciate it nonetheless," I say.

When River went to drop our mom home, her house was trashed, and the animals had been let out. Rosalind's information was correct—the Lost Lions MC had gone there to exact their revenge.

And without her giving us the heads-up, my mother might not be alive today.

Neither would Tatum, because River would have tracked him down and killed him, and probably the rest of the MC, but that's another story.

"You're welcome," she replies, clearing her throat. "I know you probably won't believe me, but there was no ulterior motive. I heard what they were planning, and the Angels MC are still my family. My father was the president before Julianna took over. I don't want my clubhouse destroyed; I have so many memories there. And I don't want anything to happen to my nephew. He hasn't done anything. He's just a child."

I feel like what she's saying is genuine, and that's coming from a person who has every reason to hate her. "Well, thank you, from all of us."

She shrugs, playing it off. "There's probably one more thing you should know," she adds, smirking.

"Oh no, what now?" I ask, frowning.

"Melinda…"

"Shit, you know everything, don't you?" I mutter, waiting for her to continue.

She laughs and leans forward against the counter. "Yes, I do. People like to gossip, especially when they come in here. You'd be surprised at the number of secrets that get spilled." She looks around. "I think it's the crystals. They make a safe space."

"Okay, well, please don't leave me in suspense any longer," I say, and she grins.

"It's not Damon's baby," she says, touching one

of the amethyst crystals in front of us. "In fact, from what I've heard, there is no baby. She wanted to trap him and is now trying to get pregnant by any random man with dark hair, to try to pin it on him."

"She's not even pregnant?" I ask, gritting my teeth. "That fucking bitch! I knew it!"

Rosalind nods sympathetically. "Nope, but she's trying so there's a baby in there when you go to the appointment."

"Wow, you're really up to date with all the local gossip."

We would have known, though, because the pregnancy would have only been a few weeks along, instead of a few months. I suppose this just brings us a lot of peace and saves me time stressing about the situation.

"Gossiping queen right here. Trust me, it's a superpower."

"I can see that. Thanks, Rosalind. I appreciate it," I say, offering her a small smile.

"He's a good man. He deserves a happily ever after," she adds.

I walk out of there with a few crystals, wanting to support her, but also being drawn in by that damn amethyst she tried to give me the first time I stepped in here.

When I get into my car, I take a moment to just feel relieved.

Our fairy tale is back on.

And I couldn't be happier.

Chapter Thirty-Nine

Damon

We end up at Devil's Play for a drink after our ride. The show doesn't start until evening, so right now it's just a bar where we can chill without any worries in the world.

"Corey is very happy," River says to me, peeling the label off his beer. "So, thank you."

"Thank you for not murdering me," is all I can manage to say back, and he laughs.

"I like you, Damon," he says back, and then we clink our drinks together, and all is good in the world.

Diamond can't stop looking at Echo, and I can't stop giving him shit about it. "Why don't you just ask her out? Corey said she's coming to the clubhouse tomorrow night—perfect opportunity."

"Is she?" he asks, perking up. "I don't know. She's just so regal and proper, and I'm a fucking ex-stripper and porn star."

I start choking, and my future brother-in-law hits me on the back. We might not have spoken about marriage yet, but there's no doubt that one day Corey is going to be my wife. "Okay, I didn't know that part."

"Must have slipped my mind," he replies, shrugging sheepishly, his eyes going back to Echo.

"A lot of slipping would have been happening," Blaze adds, laughing to himself. "Fucking hell, Diamond. Imagine if she's watching porn one day and just comes across you. If you ask her out, you should probably give her the heads-up. Not head. The heads-up," he clarifies, and we are all assholes because soon everyone is laughing.

Diamond rubs the back of his neck. "Well, not much I can do about my past. I haven't done it in a few years, if that makes it any better. And some women seem to like it."

I look over at Echo in her business attire—no-nonsense white shirt and black slacks—and wonder if she's one of those women.

I'm going to go with no.

But hey, you never know.

She comes over and looks at us. "What's the occasion?"

"We're all alive," Romeo says, lifting up his scotch.

Cheers all around.

"Corey has invited me to the clubhouse tomorrow, I hope that's okay," she checks with Romeo.

"Of course, you are always welcome," he tells her.

"It's nice you've finally decided to mix business and pleasure."

"Well, I don't know about all that," she murmurs, her eyes going to Diamond.

Interesting.

"But I'm looking forward to catching up with the girls. Corey told me not to bring anything, but I want to. Is there anything you can think of?" she asks me.

"She'd have it all handled. I bet she's gone out and bought everything already knowing her," I reply, pulling out my phone to see if she's messaged me, and she has.

Corey: I spoke to Rosalind. Word on the grapevine is Melinda isn't even pregnant, but is trying to get pregnant now.

"Motherfucker," I whisper.

Damon: I knew it! My gut was telling me that was the case, but I was trying not to be an asshole.

Corey: Not the smartest plan. The timing would be off and you'd know that. I think she's just desperate.

Damon: She has been quiet, so maybe she's decided not to continue with her scheme.

"What?" Jag asks, nosily trying to look at my screen.

I tell them what Corey said, and they all cheer again.

"I can't believe she tried to pull this on you." Romeo shakes his head, scowling. "At least I'm not the only one with a pain-in-the-ass ex…" He pauses. "Not even girlfriend. Ex-hookup."

"I just hope she lets it go and leaves me alone now," I say, swallowing down the rest of my drink quickly. "I don't need Corey to get upset again just because Melinda can't get over the fact that I've got an old lady now, and I'm not fucking her."

"Yeah, good luck with that," Romeo replies, asking Echo if he can get another round of drinks.

"Don't you guys have to ride home?" she asks skeptically, as she grabs the beers out of the fridge.

"Yeah, but we don't have to be home anytime soon," River replies, resting his arm on Romeo. "Do we?"

"I have to work. Here. Tonight," I remind them.

Echo shrugs as she slides me my beer. "Best hope that nothing goes wrong, then, right?"

"How many seats do you have in your car?" I ask her.

"Five. I can always call them a taxi, though."

We all end up staying for a few more hours and drinking many more beers. I cut myself off much earlier than them, just in case, but I'm not worried with everyone here. Anyone would be stupid to start something tonight.

Corey: Where the hell is everyone?

Damon: Devil's Play.

Corey: We're coming.

Damon: Good, you can drive us all home.

Corey: How drunk are you?

"The women are coming," I let them all know, because apparently, we are partying two nights in a row.

And I don't know about them, but I'd like nothing more than Corey here with me.

"They will be tonight," one of the men calls out, and I catch Echo rolling her eyes. No wonder she's never dated a biker—she has to sit around listening to us in our true form most nights.

They arrive an hour or so later, and Julianna has Julian with her, obviously not trusting her parents to look after him again. She doesn't drink but sits with us all and has a good time.

"You look beautiful," I tell Corey, touching the thin strap of her black dress.

"And you look like you've had one too many drinks," she replies, sitting down on my lap with her arms going around my neck. "But you still look and smell oh so good."

She puts her face into my neck, and I'm tempted to take her out back right now.

"Don't tease me," I whisper so only she can hear. "Or we'll be leaving early."

"Don't threaten me with a good time," she replies, kissing me on the cheek.

This is the first time she's been this affectionate with me in front of River, and I like how comfortable she is getting with it all. It just feels so natural with her, like this is exactly where I'm meant to be.

And she's not just my old lady.

She's my favorite person in the world.

So distracted by her, I don't notice Gio step into the room until it's too late. His gun is pointed right at River.

"Get down," I tell Corey, pushing her under the table as River stands, hands in the air as he steps forward, purposely moving away from the women, who are all ducking down. The men stay standing, forming a protective line in front of them.

"Did you think I was going to let it go that easily?" Gio smirks, stepping farther into the room. "You might need to hire some new security." He looks like shit, his jeans and shirt dirty, his hair a mess. He obviously has had a rough time, and now he's here to try to have the final word by killing River. The music still plays in the background, adding extra stimulation that I don't need right now. I get ready to reach down and grab the knife at my ankle.

"Don't do something you're going to regret,"

Romeo seethes, jaw tightening. "Put the gun down, if you want to walk out of here alive, Gio."

"Put your gun down," he growls at Romeo, who has slowly reached for his own weapon. "The Lions have turned their backs on me because I let you run me out of town. Tatum fucking hates me. And now I have nothing to lose. So, I'm going to get my revenge."

Gio pulls the trigger as River darts to the ground, and he misses. Movement out of the corner of my eye has me shocked and horrified as I see Corey stand with a gun in her hand. She shoots at Gio, and hits him in the chest.

He goes down, blood spilling out of him and onto the carpet.

Romeo rushes over and disarms him, while I turn to Corey with wide eyes. Her fingers are still shaking as they hold the weapon, and I slowly wrap my hand around hers and take it off her.

"Are you okay?" I ask, pushing her against my chest.

She nods, taking a deep, slow breath as she gathers her composure. "I'm just glad I kept that gun in my purse."

River comes up behind her and holds her. "What the fuck were you thinking?"

Her lower lip trembles. "I watched Matthew die. I wouldn't have survived losing another brother."

River slams his eyes shut and takes a deep breath, then kisses the top of her head. "You saved me. All of us. Thank you."

"He's dead," Romeo calls out.

We share a look between us.

While I'm fucking happy he's dead, I would rather it have been at someone else's hand.

Anyone else's.

But Corey is brave, strong, and resilient.

And I couldn't be prouder to call her mine.

Chapter Forty

Corey

I killed a man.

And now Damon keeps watching me with concern in those beautiful stormy gray eyes, almost waiting for me to break down over it, but I haven't. I'm not losing any more people I love, and for once in my life I was able to protect my family. Protect River.

Damon had taken me straight home afterward, while River dealt with the body. I didn't ask what they did with it. This might very well catch up with me at some point, and I know that, but I will pay whatever price I have to. For now, I distract myself by spending time with the people I killed to save.

The next night Echo comes over, and surprisingly enough so does the good doctor. Or as she introduces herself, Raine.

"Raine Shine?" I ask, remembering Romeo calling her Dr. Shine.

She winces a little, twirling her dark hair around her finger. Jag was right, she is a gorgeous woman, with dark skin, big, brown eyes, and a calm energy around her. "Yeah, my parents were hippies who thought they were funny."

I laugh, happy that she has a sense of humor. I think she'll fit right in here. "Well, Raine, it's lovely to meet you. Can I get you something to drink?"

Jag comes up next to me, butting in. "I'm pretty sure that's supposed to be my line. Nice to see you again, Dr. Shine."

I think he would love to call her doctor in the bedroom. The way his eyes are eating her up I feel like I'm intruding in a private moment, instead of just a simple conversation.

"Please, Jag, call me Raine," she replies. "And yes, I'd love a drink."

Jag steals her away, and I go and sit outside with Echo and Bella, drinks in hand, music playing in the background. I got Damon to put up more fairy lights, so the whole place is lit up. It's such a vibe.

"You made all this food yourself?" Echo asks me, eying the massive grazing platter I did up. I may have gone a little overboard, but I do love to host, and I love to feed people.

Food is my love language.

"Yes, sometimes we get caterers, but I did it all this time," I say, tilting my head to Bella. "She made all the cocktails, and the men all helped set it up. Julianna put together the playlist. It was a group effort."

"Julianna listens to Tupac?" Echo asks, sounding surprised.

"Yes, yes she does," I reply, amused. "So, what else do you do when you're not working?"

"To be honest, nothing much. I have my own house, and it's just me who lives there. My family lives in another state," she explains, sighing. "If I'm not at Devil's Play, I'm just out hanging with Rupert."

"Rupert?" I ask, thinking Diamond is going to be let down if she has a boyfriend.

"My pug," she clarifies. "And I used to love that, just living a quiet life in my own space. But recently I've just gotten over spending all my time alone, and I think I want to put myself out there and be a little more social. Not to mention I'm not getting any younger."

"Well, you came to the right place. We'd love to hang out with you more, and there are a few single men here but no single women, so the odds are in your favor. You can literally take your pick," I say, chewing on an ice cube from my cocktail. "But I think I know who you like."

"Who?" she asks, green eyes going wide. "Is this about Damon? I only hit on him once and it was before I knew you two were together. He shut me down right away, I promise."

Huh?

"Uh, I was going to say Diamond. I didn't know anything about you hitting on Damon," I say, looking over at the man in question, who is happily chatting with Leif, completely unaware that he's pissed me right off by not telling me this happened.

"I'm sorry, Corey. I would have never hit on him had I known he was taken. I'm not that kind of woman. And it was the first time I've ever hit on any of the men, so it was definitely not a good experience," she says, touching my arm so I look at her.

"No, it's okay," I say, forcing a smile. "I appreciate you telling me, but I wish that he had instead."

"He probably didn't want to ruin our friendship since it only just started," she says, defending him, which annoys me even further.

"Yeah, I know. Anyway, never mind, nothing happened and it's in the past."

And I do feel like Echo is a trustworthy woman, and I believe what she's saying. I've always heard that she stayed away from the bikers and kept the relationship very professional, so the fact that she chose Damon out of all the men in the club has me wondering if she really did like him.

"And you're right about Diamond," she says, looking over at him. "I don't know…there's something about him. We chatted a little that night you all came out. What do you know about him?"

Bella answers for me because I'm still lost in my thoughts.

"He used to be a stripper," she blurts out, then lowers her voice. "And we think a pretty damn good one."

I have to wonder how this is going to go down.

"Really?" Echo replies, studying him. "I mean, he definitely has the body for it. I don't think I'm cut out to date a sexy stripper, though. I run a burlesque house, I see how much attention these dancers get."

"Who said anything about dating?" Bella whispers, and we all laugh. Mine is a little fake, because I'm still angry.

Except then Diamond comes over and sits down with us. "What's so funny?"

"Nothing," Echo says, sitting back and crossing her legs. "Are you having a good night?"

"I am now," he replies, leaning closer to her to say something.

Bella and I slowly take our leave, and I walk right over to Damon, who playfully kisses my face and puts his arm over me.

"Damon, why didn't you tell me Echo hit on you? I mean, she didn't know we were together, so I wouldn't have held it against her, but why didn't you tell me?" I whisper.

His playful demeanor disappears, and he pulls me aside. "It was nothing—"

"What do you mean? She wanted you, that is something to me—"

"I didn't want to tell you because you had just become friends, and I didn't want you to get angry like you are right now. It would have made it awkward between you both," he says, cupping my face. "There's nothing between us. She was lonely, and I was there. It wasn't anything more than that."

"It's fine. This is what I get for choosing the hottest one in the group." I scowl, putting my hands on my hips.

He kisses my stubborn mouth. "I'm yours, nothing happened. I'm sorry, I should have told you, and I will forever tell you about any other woman that tries to get me into their bed."

"You better," I whisper to him in a deadly tone. "Or I won't tell you about every man that tries to get into mine."

Okay, no one has tried to get into mine recently, but I haven't really socialized with anyone outside of this club. And he's no longer jealous of Jag, who is now trying to get into bed with our doctor.

But he doesn't need to know that.

He thinks I'm the hottest woman ever, so he's probably assuming lots of men come after me all the time.

And I'm going to let him think that.

"Who?" he asks, stalking after me.

I ignore him and head inside, coming to a stop when I see none other than fucking Melinda standing in our kitchen.

We clearly have no security anymore after the Lost Lions MC left town. We're just letting anyone in.

"Who let you in here?" I ask her, turning to Damon in hopes he will handle this situation right now. I don't know why she's here, but I do need someone to let her know that she isn't welcome. This isn't a restaurant where people can drop in for free food and look for men to get them pregnant.

"The door was unlocked," she says, looking at him and not me. "I need money, Damon. If you give me some, I'll leave right now. Even a hundred would be good. I know you have it, so just hand it over. Look at this place," she adds, scanning the house. "You're loaded."

I look at her arms, and that's when I see the track marks. And this all makes a little more sense. She's not just a raging psychopath, she's on drugs. And she wants money for the next fix.

Oh, boy.

"Are you okay?" I ask, watching as she visibly starts to get agitated. Did Damon break her so much she turned to drugs? Or was this always a thing? "Can I get you something?"

"Just money," she says, hands on her stomach. "For the baby. I need to get food and things."

I'll bet.

"So you're still going with that," Damon comments, stepping in front of me. Does he think she will try to do something to me?

I walk over to Raine and whisper the situation in her ear.

She comes over right away to help, except that sets Melinda off, and she starts throwing things around the kitchen in a rage.

"Should we just give her money and lock our doors?" I ask.

Julianna storms in, not taking any of Melinda's shit, and grabs her by the arm, dragging her outside. Raine and Damon follow behind. I know he'd feel some kind of responsibility for her and wouldn't want to leave the women to handle it.

"I feel bad for her," I say to Leif, who comes over to see what is going on.

"Don't let her ruin your night—they'll take care of her," he says, pulling me back inside. He gets me on the dance floor and starts busting a move like nothing happened. What the hell? I take a tequila shot and join him.

Chapter Forty-One

Damon

We get Melinda to the hospital, but there's nothing much else we can do. I didn't even know she used hard-core dugs like that, at least she wasn't for that short time I was seeing her. What a mess. I have to look at the positives, though: at least she's not carrying my child. She admitted as much on the way there. She really was just desperate for money to buy her latest fix, and after her money ran out she knew we had lots of it, and decided to make her play. Lucky for us, Julianna wasn't drinking tonight, and drove us there and back.

The party is still cranking when we return, and Corey is on the dance floor with Echo, Bella, Leif, and Diamond. I'm glad she's not holding a grudge against Echo, which is why I didn't tell her, but I can understand why she'd be upset that I didn't. I should have. And next time I'm just going to go with straight-up honesty.

I come up behind her and she melts into me, straight away knowing that it's me. "Everything all good?"

"Yeah, she went to the hospital. Hopefully she doesn't come back here."

Julianna gave her an earful, so I don't think that she will. Raine also told her that she can come and see her at the hospital if she ever needs anything, which was very sweet of her. I just don't like how we all got dragged into Melinda's issues, but at the same time I do feel sympathetic toward her. She is someone's daughter and I hope she gets the help she needs.

Corey spins around and dances against me, her beautiful body in rhythm with the music. And after a few drinks Diamond finally doesn't hold back, showing off his moves for Echo.

As long as it's not for Corey, I don't care.

I see Echo look at Corey and mouth *Oh my god* as he gyrates around, body rolling and sensually teasing all of the women here with his skills.

Looking over at Romeo, I see him covering Julianna's eyes, who is trying to move away from him to see.

And of course then they have to put "Pony" back on again.

I dance the rest of the night away with Corey, lost in each other, surrounded by our family.

I went from a foster kid no one wanted to adopt, to this.

Life couldn't get any better.

A few days later a letter comes for Corey, and it's from her mom. She reads it and then hands it to me.

Corey, thank you for the painting. I can see why it reminds you of Matthew, and that now he is free. I hung it up on my wall. I know we haven't always had the best relationship, and I'm sorry. I'm not perfect, and I do love you. Mom

Corey smiles but doesn't say anything else. She's in a good place, one where it doesn't matter what anyone else says about her, they don't hold any power. She knows her worth.

"That was a beautiful painting," is all I say to her, and her face lights up.

"Thank you. I'm glad she saw it for what it was." She pauses, and adds, "And I'm glad you see me for who I am."

The best decision I ever made was taking a gamble on this woman.

Epilogue

Damon

Two Years Later

Standing in the pool of our clubhouse, I grip Corey's hips, the material of her red bikini sliding along my fingers. All of us merging together here has been the best thing we've ever done, and after a year of us all living together, the MC is stronger than ever. Julianna won her fight for equality, and finally women are allowed to become official members. Although we're still protective as hell, we include them in everything we can without putting them in too much danger.

Corey turns and wraps her arms around my neck. I have to lower my head so she can reach. "If no one else was around right now I would lift you up and fuck you right here," I whisper against the shell of her ear.

"Mmm," she murmurs, sliding her fingers down my back.

"Don't mind us, we like the show!" Blaze calls out, smirking. I make a mental note to kick his ass later.

Dr. Shine strolls out from inside, handing Jag a beer and sitting down next to him. How he got her, I will never know.

"You'll just have to wait until we get back to our room," Corey replies, amusement dancing in her eyes.

I can't remember a time when I've ever been this happy.

We've spoken about maybe having a baby in the next few years, but Corey is still not sure what she wants, and I'm okay with that. A life with her is more than enough for me.

A pregnant Bella swims over to us, a glass of lemonade in her hand. "I know River is your brother-in-law now, but he will still kill you if you keep touching her like that in front of everyone."

Corey rolls her eyes and places her hand on my chest, the big oval-shaped diamond sparkling in the sun. "River can get over it; I'm a married woman now."

Unable to help myself, I kiss her slowly, savoring the moment.

Echo and Diamond join us, the bastard splashing us all as he jumps in.

Corey opens her arms and takes Julian from Julianna, sliding him into the water. Leaning back against the pool's edge, I watch everyone and smile to myself.

This is wealth.

Loyalty.

My beautiful wife.

My found family.

I couldn't have asked for anything more.

* * * * *

Acknowledgments

A big thank-you to Carina Press for working with me on this series!

Thank you to Kimberly Brower, my amazing agent, for having my back in all things. We make a great team, always have and always will.

Brenda Travers—Thank you so much for all that you do to help me. I am so grateful. You go above and beyond and I appreciate you so much.

Tenielle—Baby sister, I don't know where I'd be without you. You are my rock. Thanks for all you do for me and the boys. We all adore you and appreciate you. I might be older, but you inspire me every day. When I grow up, I want to be like you.

Sasha—Baby sister, do you know one of the things that I love about you? You are you. You don't care what anyone else thinks, you stay true to yourself and I am so proud of you. Tahj reminds me of you in that way. Never change. I love you.

Christian—Thank you for always being there for

me, and for accepting me just the way I am. Thank you for trying to understand me. We are so different, opposites in every way, but I think that's the balance that we both need. I always tell you how lucky you are to have me in your life, but the truth is I'm pretty damn lucky myself. I appreciate all you do for me and the boys. I love you.

Mum and Dad—Thank you for always being there for me and the boys no matter what. And thank you, Mum, for making reading such an important part of our childhood. I love you both!

Natty—My bestie soulmate, thank you for being you. For knowing me so well, and loving me anyway. I hope Mila sees this book one day and knows Aunty Chanty loves her so much!

Ari—Thank you for still being there for me, ten years later. You are one of the best humans I've ever known.

To my three sons, I'm so proud of the men you are all becoming, and I love you all so very much. I hope that watching me work hard every day and following my dreams inspires you all to do the same. I love every second of being your mother. You will forever be my greatest blessings.

Chookie—No, I love you more.

Tahj—You make me so proud. You are silently protective of everyone around you. You are smart, and creative. I see you.

Ty—You'll be happy to know I've finished my "working shenanigans" deadline. Love you.

And to my readers, thank you for loving my words. I hope this book is no exception.